our brothers

at the bottom of the

bottom of the sea

JONATHAN DAVID KRANZ

our brothers
at the bottom of the
bottom of the sea

Henry Holt and Company
New York

Henry Holt and Company, LLC
Publishers since 1866
175 Fifth Avenue
New York, New York 10010
macteenbooks.com

Library of Congress Cataloging-in-Publication Data
Kranz, Jonathan.
    Our brothers at the bottom of the bottom of the sea / Jonathan David Kranz. —
First edition.
            pages   cm
    Summary: In their search for answers about their brothers' mysterious deaths,
two teenagers in a small seaside vacation town will discover just how far a man will
go to protect his kingdom.
    ISBN 978-1-62779-050-5 (hardback) — ISBN 978-1-62779-051-2 (e-book)
[1. Brothers and sisters—Fiction. 2. Death—Fiction.] I. Title.
    PZ7.1.K73Ou 2015   [Fic]–dc23   2014043029

Henry Holt books may be purchased for business or promotional use.
For information on bulk purchases, please contact the Macmillan
Corporate and Premium Sales Department at (800) 221-7945 x5442
or by e-mail at specialmarkets@macmillan.com.

First edition—2015 / Designed by April Ward
Printed in the United States of America by R. R. Donnelley & Sons Co.,
Harrisonburg, Virginia

10 9 8 7 6 5 4 3 2 1

This story is dedicated to the
strong women in my life: my wife,
Eileen, but especially my daughters,
Rebecca and Anastasia, who in their
youth have, like Rachel, shown the
world the lion hearts of the brave.

our brothers

at the bottom of the

bottom of the sea

aftermath

The beach was the one spot the police and fire crews could not close to crowds attracted to the flames. People gathered on the sand, summoned by an ember sky and the pillows of white smoke riding through Sea Town. It was after midnight, and the crowd had the matted, tossed-together quality of people hastily roused from sleep and dressed in whatever had been close by: pajama bottoms, loose shorts, oversize T-shirts, and zippered hoodies. Mostly, they watched Happy World burn in silence, hugging themselves against the cold night air. Children clung to their parents' pant legs, and grown men and women covered their mouths, trapping gasps behind their hands. The air crackled with bullhorn commands and the popping of heat-splintered wood. The crowd seemed immobilized by its fascination. When the tide crawled up the beach, the onlookers closest to the ocean were startled, as if the sudden water were hands that had reached out low and cold to grab them by the ankles.

In front of the amusement park's castle facade of arched

entryways and rampart towers, firefighters in yellow slickers heaved lines of fire hose. Arcs of water shot up and out from glittering chrome nozzles, desperately pushing against risers of flame that refused to back down. The fire punched through the castle clapboards in glowing vines twisting up and around the guardian towers, illuminating the sentries, the brass buttons of their uniforms, and the steel blades of their bayonets. In mute empathy the crowd drew closer together, fixated on the toy soldiers' impending doom.

A bullhorn roared, and at once the yellow slickers fell back. Firelogged clumps of clapboard dropped from the walls, raining down on the boardwalk below. The collective sympathy of the crowd turned toward a dark brute on the ground, a fiberglass bear with its arms raised to welcome guests at the central gate. In a matter of seconds, a bonfire of debris had encircled the bear; the gesture that for years had beckoned guests now became a plea for help, begging escape from the flames.

The crowd, both horrified and fascinated, could no longer remain silent; bursts of protest, first in whispers, then in shouts, rose from the onlookers. "No way." "This can't be happening." "No."

At the far edge of the witnessing mass, two young people stood apart, a pale girl in a baseball cap, a black boy with a restless Afro that shook in the breeze. Her head was on his shoulder, as if taking shelter under his hair.

"Look," she said. An entire wall peeled away, a hot and impatient flower of fire that came crashing down, taking sentries and turrets and flag posts with it. The collapse exposed a skeleton of black steel and smoking strings of loose cable, and buried the bear for good.

"You know what happens now?" the young man said. "Everyone's going to say, 'This is our 9/11, the day Happy World burned down.' There'll be posters and T-shirts: 'August 14, 2014. Always remember.'" He squeezed his companion's fingers. "They're going to come for us," he said. "We should go. Now."

"No," she said. "Too suspicious."

"What about Ethan? You think he—"

"No."

"Glad you're so sure. He probably thinks it was you. You think he'll say so?" When she didn't respond, he added, "They'll look for enemies."

"Then they'll be looking the wrong way."

He searched her face. "You know who did this?"

"Maybe," she said, drawing her arm around him. "Sledge Leary?"

"I wish. But this ain't a comic book," he said. "Seriously. Is it someone close to us?"

"Close to us?"

With the collapse of the Happy World facade, the fire, as if it had run out of rage, began to dim. Rolls of black smoke replaced the flames, and the beach crowds began to disperse.

"Close to us?" the girl said again. "Yes and no."

following the script

Rachel did not know where she would find what she was looking for, or even what exactly she needed to find, but she was fairly certain that once she got beyond the seasonal displays of inflatable toys and neon boogie boards, she would find the homely, useful things that should be the true business of a hardware store. This one had low-hanging fluorescent fixtures and the sour smell of weed killer and burlap sacks. Like a houseguest searching for a bathroom, Rachel peeked uncertainly down the aisles. The signs suspended from the ceiling were only marginally helpful. She wished for something explicit, like "stuff you need to fix a hole in the wall."

An employee in a store apron approached Rachel, examining her as if anticipating customer needs was one of his chores. Rachel did not appreciate the attention. In general, she dressed for invisibility. She wore loose cargo pants and a white sweatshirt that sagged from her torso like a spent balloon. A blue baseball cap, with a strip of duct tape covering the sports logo, crowned her shoulder-length brown hair. Her canvas sneakers, which were originally bright blue, were now dishwater gray.

"Looking for something?" he asked.

"I need to fix a hole. In a wall."

"Drywall?"

"Yeah, it's dry." She felt a little defensive. She and Betty had at least a baseline level of competency, enough to keep the damn walls from getting wet.

The man crossed his arms over his chest and smiled. "I mean," he said with mock patience, "is it Sheetrock or plaster?"

"I don't know. It's a wall."

"Ohh-kay," he said. "How big is this hole?"

About the size of a man's fist. Not a particularly large man, nor even an especially angry man, but a frustrated man who had run out of things to say and, not wanting to leave without having the last word, had made his concluding argument in the wall.

"About the size of a doughnut," Rachel said.

"The doughnut hole or the whole doughnut?"

"The whole. The whole doughnut, I mean."

"Good," the man said. "I'm glad we're being scientific about this." He ticked off the necessary items on his fingers. "You'll need a ten-inch knife, maybe a six-inch knife, a patch kit, some mud, a mud pan—"

"Mud?"

"Joint compound." He rubbed at a dirt spot on his apron. "You know, it might be easier to get help, have someone do this for you."

It wouldn't, Rachel thought. The guy who had left the hole

in the wall was the plumber Betty had called in to fix a leaky faucet. That was a month and many noisy nights ago. The faucet still dripped, just not as much.

"We'll do it ourselves," she said.

"Then you'll need the right tools." He motioned Rachel to step aside and, while she waited, harvested the necessary items from the shelves. They made an expensive-looking pile at the counter. The man scanned them into the register, and Rachel admired the point-of-sale displays: key rings, candy-colored miniature flashlights, and little pocket knives, too adorable to be either effective tools or weapons, which would fit comfortably into a purse or pocket—which, Rachel thought, would fit very comfortably in her hand.

With Curtis, taking things had been easy. He was a walking distraction, a goodwill magnet who attracted many fans, mostly women, but men too, who threw affection on him as readily as the devout pinned dollars on parade saints. While Curtis plucked their heartstrings, Rachel plucked their tabletops, their counters, their shelves. At home, she had a dresser drawer full of cosmetics she would never use, a closet rack of clothes she'd never wear—that was beside the point. The point was a little in the having, a lot in the taking, but not at all in the using.

Now there was this man standing right in front of her, no more than two, maybe three, feet away. That would be cutting it close. But, Rachel believed, the distance between two people could hardly be reduced to a matter of inches. "You have the number of a good handyman?" she asked.

"After I just rung all this in?"

She smiled. "You might be right. I might need help. Just in case."

"You have seven days for returns," he said, turning toward a drawer behind him, "if you have the receipt and the stuff isn't used." While he rummaged for the right business card, Rachel picked an emerald green folding knife from the display, slipping it into the cargo pocket of her pants, where it hung weighty and full, like a ripe piece of fruit.

Under Rachel's bare feet, the sand shifted damp and cool. Betty, satisfied with the dark, said it was time, and they crossed the beach toward the water's edge. Betty carried the pillowcase full of shells—she insisted on it—and Rachel carried their footwear and a loose sheet of paper that shuddered in the breeze. The board-walk world receded behind them, a blade of bright lights between the black sky above and the night-dark beach beneath it. Crashing surf overwhelmed most of the carnival chatter on the boards.

"You couldn't have . . . you know?" Betty said, sweeping her free hand up and down her body to signify the clothing on Rachel's.

"It's what I always wear," Rachel said.

"That's what I mean. Just for today, I mean."

The Big Day. While Rachel had patched the wall, Betty said they had turned a corner. It had been a bad year, and they needed a fresh start. To close one door and open another, they would return Curtis's shells to the sea. They had spent the last hour working on a memorial in the kitchen, Betty dictating the mean-ing she was looking for while Rachel found ways to put that meaning into words. They wrote about returning home, about finding a way forward, about an end that was a new beginning.

Rachel wasn't entirely sold on the script, but it didn't mat-ter: Betty bought it. In any event, she could hardly read it.

"You bring a flashlight?" Betty asked.

"No," Rachel said. She regretted her missed opportunity at the hardware store, the handy miniature flashlight she could have taken instead of the pretty knife.

"Shit. Can you read it anyway?"

"I'll try."

"Good girl."

Rachel parked their shoes side by side in the sand, and the two walked to the edge of the surf, Rachel now holding on to the script with both hands to keep it from being ripped free by the wind. She looked out over the waves but did not think about Curtis or his shells or memory—she looked ahead, anticipating how good it would feel to be in a time and place where all this would be something behind them, the wake sliding back from their boat.

As if.

"You think it's enough?" Betty asked.

"What?"

"Are we just going to dump them here? Shouldn't there be more to it?" Betty shielded her eyes against a sun that was not there, saluting the dark.

She was looking for signs, Rachel thought. A kind word from the wind, a nod from the moon. Maybe something she could see, but more important, something she could feel. Betty expected something that hadn't yet arrived. Rachel needed to break the paralysis. "We could throw them," she said. It might be satisfying, grabbing a handful of Curtis's old shells and flinging them into the waves. It had been a big step just removing them from her room, which she had shared with Curtis—he hadn't been able to sleep without her. There were shells on every available horizontal surface—on the dresser, on the windowsills, on Rachel's vanity, where like soldiers, they had surrounded her hairbrush.

"Mom," Rachel said, "we can't just stand here."

"Over there," Betty said, pointing to a jagged ridge of seaweed-slick boulders jutting out from the shore into the waves. White curls of water smacked against their sides, sending up leaps of sea spray. "We'll pour them from up top. Make an offering of them."

"I don't know," Rachel said. At the far end of the jetty, mounted low to the rocks between two crossed red flags, a white steel sign shook in the wind. DANGER, it said in blunt capital letters. The sign was new. Last winter, a teenage boy had slipped from the top of the jetty and cracked his head, drowning in the water below. People talked about why and how, and the town responded by putting up a sign.

"We'll just have to be careful, that's all," Betty said.

"Mom . . ."

"C'mon. Less talking, more doing." The words faded in and out as Betty released them, eaten by the wind. There was no point in arguing. Betty started for the jetty, and Rachel followed through the wet sand to the slick stones. They climbed awkwardly, making handholds in the empty air to balance themselves, crabbing their way over the cold stones, squishy with bladderwort and sea lettuce. Several times Rachel slipped, forcing an odd dance of swinging arms and jerking legs to regain her footing. Betty, walking confidently a few yards ahead, seemed more stable.

Just feet from the sign, shoulder to shoulder on the rocks, they were getting hammered by bursts of salt spray. "We'll have to make this quick," Rachel said, yelling into Betty's ear.

With the sack clamped between her knees, Betty crossed herself. "Let's get started."

It was almost impossible to see, impossible to hold the paper still. Rachel improvised, merging what she could read with what she remembered and what she could make up on the spot. "We come to this place—"

"Is that what it says?"

"Yes!"

"Don't we start with something about God?"

"Oh, God," Rachel said, "we come to this place, a place Curtis loved, to remember and to honor and to hope." From the boardwalk, the PinDrop exhaled a deep, hydraulic sigh.

"Go on."

"To hope and to return"—she nodded at Betty, and Betty opened the sack—"to return what Curtis loved to the place he loved," Rachel continued. She suddenly pictured her brother with his hand squirreling down his shorts—a not infrequent occurrence—and suppressed a smile. That was a love with no place to return to.

"The place he loved," Betty repeated, looking around as if admiring the water, the waves, the jetty, for the first time. Rachel looked too, hoping this would be a last time, thinking how wonderful it would be to see it all like objects in a rearview mirror, diminishing with distance.

Betty grabbed Rachel's shoulder. Rachel thought she was about to slip, but Betty pointed to the sign between the crossed flags. "Look," she said.

"I told you it was dangerous," Rachel shouted.

"It's a sign," Betty said, almost inaudibly.

"Of course it's a sign."

"Look."

Beneath DANGER, someone had added in a sloping, elementary school print, *Don't fall.*

Betty clamped a hand over her mouth as if preventing a prisoner there from escaping.

"It's just a coincidence," Rachel said. "It doesn't mean anything."

Betty shook her head.

"It doesn't mean a damn thing. We're almost done. We'll finish this, and then . . . then we can move on."

"We can't. Not now."

"Why not?" Rachel asked. "Because of the sign? Because of some stupid words?"

But Betty had already slung the sack of shells over her shoulder and was mince-footing her way over the rocks to the shore.

"Give them to me, then. I'll do it by myself."

"You can't," Betty shouted from the beach end of the rocks. "This isn't a by-yourself kind of thing."

"Why not?"

"Family," Betty said, wiggling her feet into her sandals. "The ties that bind."

When it suits you, Rachel thought. She wadded the memorial into a ball and threw it into the water, watching it bob like a little doll's head before it was overcome by the waves and drawn down into the sea.

May 17, 2013

You get the best views from the crest of the Ferris wheel: rooftop air-compressor assemblies; cooling fins, stacked like steel toast, at the power transfer station; the long narrow ghost of the railroad right-of-way where the tracks used to be, years ago, when tourists came here by train. They come by the carload now. Next week, the roads that stretch out like frayed wire will be jammed with minivans. Next week, Happy World will open for the season.

This week, Walter and I have to get things ready. This is the time of year Walter hates the most. There are a thousand details leaning on him, and one big boss bearing down. He's the classic Happy World employee. Forget Happy World "magic"—experience has made Walter a believer in Happy World power, the power of stone. Today, after a couple of test runs of the wheel, I asked Walter to let me on for a preview of the ride. He wasn't crazy about the idea. "Stone's already got my nuts in a sling, and I promise you, they don't need any company." But I was persistent: if it wasn't safe for me, how could we open it to the public? That was hardly Walter's concern. He wanted what was safe for him.

I told him that one way or another, I was riding the wheel—we could be quick about it or we could stand around and argue all day. Every minute Walter wasted with me was a minute denied to a cold beer and a bag of Fritos. The loss was too much to bear. He gave his trademark lookout glance over his shoulder and told me to keep my head down. I got a gondola to myself and a radio, just in case. It was too noisy, crackling with grounds crew arguments over restroom duties and overtime. I turned it off.

Which was just as well. In the quiet, I could hear the hum of the motor, the whine of the capstan wheels, the regular clickety-clack of meshing gears and chain links. Then I felt something out of place, more an intuitive buzz than a distinct sensation. I licked my fingers and rested them on the mounting brackets of the gondola. Vibration. Definitely. You'd expect some resonance on a windy day, but the air was still—the banners over the park turrets hardly moved.

No, this was mechanical. And I hadn't felt it before. When I got off the ride, Walter was white as a sheet. Stone stood behind him with his arms folded. Trouble.

I shouldn't have been on the wheel before the inspector's approval. Especially since I won't turn eighteen for another two months and am technically a minor. But Stone knows I'm discreet. And I've come in handy many times before. I climbed out of the car and said there was vibration.

Stone said maybe it was my cell phone. Did I keep it in my pants? He laughed, then Walter laughed too.

I didn't let them get to me. I suggested we get a stethoscope and listen to the bearings. "Vibration," I said, quoting the reference manuals, "is often the first sign of mechanical failure."

Stone wasn't impressed, but he didn't go ballistic, either. He rolled his eyes and said he had three engineers on his payroll who were paid way too much money to fuck around with stethoscopes. They've run the tests, he insisted, and the wheel was good to go.

But I wouldn't let it go. I asked if they had listened to the bearings.

If looks could kill, Walter's would've knocked me dead. I'm sure he would've settled for shutting me up. Having lost face, he was looking for the easiest way to kiss ass. "When they say it's good, it's good," he said.

Stone squinted into the sky as if reading the clouds. "If you can feel vibrations a hundred feet up in the air, there's a whole different set of bearings that need to be checked," he said.

I said it wouldn't hurt to look.

Stone told me I needed to look for a girlfriend. "At your age, everything feels like it's vibrating."

For my money, Walter enjoyed the joke far too much. I pushed the radio into his hands and walked away. Machines can be fixed. People are another story.

wwjd?

Chilly temperatures and gray skies covered a beach abandoned to shivering lifeguards in windbreakers, their knees cuddled up to their chins, and spindly little birds picking at the sand. Overhead, squawking gulls, fighting over scraps of fried dough, echoed a collective mood of disappointment. It was a summer day gone wrong, and that felt just right for Ethan. He tugged his hood down to the bridge of his sunglasses—his favorite pair of mirrored aviators—then buckled his hands in the front pouch of his pullover sweatshirt. He owned a half dozen hoodies he preferred, but today, he'd picked a white one without logos or lettering, cool and anonymous.

Ethan smiled because he was no longer Ethan Waters: he was a mystery man with determination in his heart and a map in his pocket. The latter, carefully scribed the evening before with a school ruler and a sharp pencil, was hardly necessary; he knew the boardwalk inside and out. But as his friend Garrett would say, *It's about form. There's a way of doing things, and if you're going to do them, you got to do them the right way.* Even though making the map took an hour of unnecessary time—Ethan drawing the thing on a sheet of plate glass, just like in the movies, so that his work would no leave no detectable indentations behind—and the map would never be consulted while he was actually engaged in his mission (too conspicuous), it served a purpose. Should he ever choose to let Garrett or anyone else in on his secret, he could stand up to his cross-examination and say truthfully that he had fulfilled his mission according to form, in all the right ways.

The poor weather played into Ethan's plan, thinning out the boardwalk crowds and distracting the tourists who remained. They hustled along the walk with quick steps and downcast eyes that would not notice anything unusual, even if the unusual was uncoiling just inches from their cones of soft-serve ice cream, their cardboard boats of vinegar fries.

Ethan climbed the Thirteenth Street boardwalk ramp, congratulating himself for his plan's balance of cunning and simplicity. It was exactly the kind of effort Jason might admire, an act that required calculated intelligence and a little bit of courage— but not too much. Jason had stood a full head taller than Ethan, lean and cool, measuring the world through precise, marble-gray eyes that always did the math.

"You don't think things through," Jason used to say in his most annoying older-brother voice. Today, Ethan would prove him wrong. At the top of the ramp, he paused, gripping the thick, felt-tipped marker he had pocketed before he left the house. The surf, which, on the beach, practically roared into the sand, merely hummed like radio static when you were on the boardwalk, a humbled equal to the gulls, the crowds, the hissing amusement park rides. The wind slapped a runaway flyer against Ethan's ankle, a promotion for Happy World's latest attraction—the Thruster—cluttered with exclamation points and delirious screaming mouths. He crumpled it into a ball and tossed it in a trash barrel.

A cluster of high school girls crossed Ethan's path in overly optimistic clothing—shorts, spaghetti-strap tops, flip-flops that slapped the wood boards. With some alarm, he saw Garrett's right-hand man, Mitchell, trailing behind them, his Labrador-black hair falling over his eyes as he followed the scent of girl, girl, girl. Ethan turned away, concealing himself behind his hood, watching them parade past and hoping that Mitchell's presence would not be a sign that Garrett was close behind. He waited, they passed, and Garrett did not show. It was just Mitchell, freelance, playing lover boy to girls who might giggle among themselves but wouldn't give him the time of day. He didn't seem to mind, and that amazed Ethan.

But the important thing wasn't Mitchell the fool but the mission ahead. Ethan, still giving his friend and the objects of his fascination wide berth, assessed his own progress so far. He had started from the north moving south, maintaining a low profile by keeping his appearances on the boardwalk to a minimum, leaving after each hit for the adjacent streets before reemerging on the walk near his preselected targets—a tactical consideration Jason would've approved. First, he had hit Happy World, tagging the wall above the water fountains in the rest area. Then he targeted the notice boards on the music pier near Eighth Street, the information kiosk at Tenth, and the covered seating area for smokers near Eleventh Street and the Pirate's Playground. Gaining confidence, he had tagged the Sizzleator, a fried food place even he found disgusting, making his mark under the counter as he pretended to tie his shoes, a clever touch that gave him a tingle of pride—who said he wasn't creative?

From there, he made his bravest move yet, marching down the Pirate's Playground alley to the fiberglass mascot, a pirate in red-and-white-striped pants and sagging boots, his boarding ax raised high—a meeting of the bold, Ethan thought. When he was confident the girl in the ticket booth wasn't looking, Ethan attacked the exposed belly of white pirate shirt just begging to be marked.

One target remained: the men's room he now approached from the Thirteenth Street ramp. On the map in his pocket, this final destination was marked appropriately with a capital *M*. It occurred to him that if someone read the same map upside down—and there was no compass rose to indicate north or south, up or down—that same *M* would be a *W* and would indicate exactly the wrong place to go. It didn't matter. The map was for people who would never see it anyway. Ethan's heart beat triumphantly. Had he executed his mission at night, after the boardwalk had officially closed at eleven, he would have attracted the attention of police officers riding electric three-wheelers, humming along the boards or racing across the packed sand above the surf line. Now, just before noon on a discouraging summer day, he was what he was supposed to be—just another bored kid hanging out. Not doing anything in particular.

Nothing noteworthy in that.

Ethan entered the men's room, sliding his sunglasses into his sweatshirt pocket, eyes blinking in the sudden, cinder-block gloom. Above the sinks, a fluorescent fixture crackled spastically. The dim room smelled of urinal cakes, tart and fruity. He scanned the floor—no feet in the stalls. That was good. He slipped into the nearest stall and closed the door behind him, shifting the latch shut. Facing the door, almost eye level to its hook, he took out his marker. As he pulled the cap free, it made a popping noise much louder than he had anticipated. He paused, listening. But other than the crackling light, there wasn't a sound—he was alone. He pressed the tip to the door, savoring the clean, wet strokes against the smooth, cooperative steel. In crisp block letters, his message seemed to write itself, the marker squeaking softly with each stroke, the red ink stinking of ammonia. *Don't fall,* he read, as if the words had always been there, as if he hadn't applied them himself, as if they had emerged here and everywhere else from a plain, irrepressible truth neither he nor anyone else could deny, cover, or bury. To admire the words from an even broader perspective, he stepped backward and banged his bare calves against the toilet, nearly falling over. He was glad no one was there to see that.

He tagged the two remaining stalls. Still, no one came in. When he finished, marker returned to pocket, he felt torn between the prudent need to get off the boardwalk, away from the scene of his crimes, and an urgent need to pee; he hadn't gone to the bathroom since he had begun his mission with a Mountain Dew two hours earlier. He picked the urinal at the far left of three and took aim at the cake.

Now that the mission was over, Ethan felt diminished, sad. The essence of his plan was secrecy, but the same secrecy denied him the satisfaction of telling his friends, of seeing the small awe in Mitchell's eyes, the envy Garrett would try to conceal by making his big talk even bigger. Ethan was thinking that the best, most exciting part of his summer would remain tragically unknown when the sharp squawk of a radio drew his attention to the restroom entrance. There, silhouetted by a rim of daylight, a broad-shouldered mass as ominous and indistinct as a shadow filled the doorway. Ethan squinted. Between himself and the only exit stood a police officer in a navy blue shirt packed with the paraphernalia of authority: badge, radio, pen, and pad. Had the officer followed him? Had someone tipped him off? Had Ethan done something to give himself away? In a flash, he envisioned his escape, a bold dash across the boardwalk, down the ramp, and into the back alleys, where he stood a good chance of losing anyone whose advantage in size would become a disadvantage in speed.

What would Jason do? He would say running was ridiculous, out of the question, even if Ethan somehow managed to get past an officer who was nearly as big around as a harbor buoy. And Jason would have been right. Once, two summers ago, as Ethan trailed his father around Happy World, his shoulder had been clipped from behind, nearly tumbling him across the Tea Cup railing. Turning, he came face-to-face with a teen in a ripped denim jacket, the boy's eyes wild with panic, his hands steadying Ethan apologetically by the shoulders. The boy opened his mouth as if to say something, but a burst of shouts sent him running recklessly, arms and legs flying out from him as he turned first one way, then another, until he cornered himself between the flume ride and a row of porta-johns. Within seconds, Happy World was swarming with cops; like iron filings to a magnet, they fell upon the boy, now the hidden center within a storm of arms, truncheons, and a flash of silver handcuffs. There were screams and shouts, but it was hard to tell which came from the desperate teen and the cops enclosing him, and which were the natural cries of a crowd having fun. Ethan watched, horrified and fascinated, until his father pulled him aside, out of the dark corner and into the brighter light, where park patrons had no idea of the beating being unleashed just a dozen yards away. Ethan feared he might get sick, and the feeling must have been visible on his face. "Don't worry," his father had assured him. "He won't get away."

Fortunately, this police officer hardly glanced at Ethan before choosing the urinal on his right, taking what seemed like forever to unzip his fly. With his free hand, he lowered the volume on his radio, braced in a pouch beside his service pistol.

All the adventure had evaporated. Instead, there was fear—and worse, an emptiness where anticipation had been. Jason wouldn't have been impressed by all this; he would've been disgusted. There was nothing clever about writing on a wall, and being caught doing it was even more stupid. Ethan just wanted to retreat home without incident; there, a bag of chips, the living room couch, and a cartoon program would settle him. He flushed the urinal and, with as much nonchalance as he could fake, washed his hands at the sink where no one could notice they were shaking. Somehow, the warm, soapy water was encouraging—he was coming clean. In a few moments, he would be in the clear. He dared lift his eyes to the mirror; with a shrug of his shoulders and a quick zip, the officer was finishing his business. Ethan dried his hands and started for the door, balling his used paper towel and tossing it casually into the trash can. He was just three steps from getting away.

"Hey, kid," the officer said sharply.

Ethan stopped, turning around with his hands frozen in his sweatshirt pouch. His ears seemed to swell with heat. *Come on,* he thought. *What would Jason do?*

"What's going on?" the officer asked, pointing to Ethan's sweatshirt. "You bleeding?"

Ethan looked down; there was a red stain about the size and shape of a bloodshot eye on the front of his sweatshirt. For a split second, he panicked—he had taken a hit! But by what, and how and when, he had no idea. Then he realized something worse: he had forgotten to replace the cap on his marker.

"No," Ethan said. "Just tomato sauce, I guess. I just had a slice. Of pizza."

The officer leaned in for a closer look. "There's nothing home-made about that sauce," he said. "Is that Tommasi's? You'd think they'd know better, being Italian and all. But you don't go to the boardwalk for fine dining, do you?" He flicked the stain with his index finger and rose to his full height, meeting Ethan's eyes, inspecting, it seemed, every feature on his face. Ethan could smell an undercurrent of coffee on his breath and over that, the sharp scent of spearmint chewing gum. "Aren't you Chuck Waters's kid?"

"Yeah."

"Thought I saw a resemblance," the officer said brightly, congratulating himself on his powers of observation. But then his face fell, as if recalling something unpleasant.

Ethan checked the doorway. He had a shot, if he moved quickly. But what was the point? Where would he go that he wouldn't be found? He was spotted, he was known, he was trapped.

"I'm sorry," the officer said, turning aside to wash at the sinks. "About your brother."

"Me too," Ethan said. He capped the marker within his pocket, waiting to hear anything else the officer might want to say. But there was nothing more. The radio barked back to life, the officer mumbled a few words to the handset clipped to his shoulder, and with a swiftness Ethan hadn't expected from a man of his size, he stepped through the doorway, turned to the right, and disappeared. Between the officer's stride from sink to sunlight, Ethan had been tempted to hold out his wrists. *Get out the cuffs*, he wanted to say. *Make me talk.* But the officer was gone, and Ethan stood alone by the sinks, pulling his hood up over his head.

No one had captured Ethan Waters.

May 24, 2013

My summer job search has come to its suckwad conclusion.
I was hoping for the maintenance crew. I would've
settled for ride operator. I got the Moon Walk Mini Golf.
Mini golf.

What's the deal? I asked my dad. He pretended he
didn't understand.

I told him what we both knew was the truth: I knew
the rides better than half his engineers, maybe all of
them. And what's my reward? The mini golf.

He looked up from his desk and said maybe I didn't
know as much as I thought I did. Our eyes met. When I
didn't look away, he said his maintenance guys had to
be certified.

Please. I've been telling these guys what to do for
years. Who found the axle fault on the Billy Goat? The
water pump failure on the Log Hill Flume? The
malfunctioning armature on the Twirl n' Spill? The

certified guys? The guys with a piece of paper in their files and a few hours of classes to their credit? If a mechanical failure jumped up and bit them on the ass, hard, they might find one. But I wouldn't put money on it.

I brought up the Thruster. That was the big whoop-de-do this year, the exciting new ride that would pull in the crowds. For all the hype, the Thruster was basically a large letter "U" with a launcher at the base: riders rocketed up the track to the peak of one side as if being sent off the rail and into space. At the last few feet, just before the precipice and the prospect of sailing, carriage and all, into the sea, the carriage brakes to a lurching, head-snapping stop. Then it rolls backward, past the base and up the back half of the track, before it settles at the bottom again. All in all, no more than thirty seconds from launch to dismount. But we expect it to inspire long lines of customers—and it cost Stone a bundle.

My dad said the Thruster only made things worse. "Money's tight."

But the mini golf? Couldn't he have pulled for me? Didn't he have influence? I asked. He's Stone's right-hand man after all. Shouldn't that count for something?

There was something rigid about my dad's face and hands, as if someone had just turned a ratchet in his back and drawn his skin together, that made me regret my words. Dad said he had a stack of applications two inches thick, and that I got more than most kids got. "You want the job or not?"

What could I say? I don't go to Carnegie Mellon for another three months, and I'm not going to hang around Ethan all summer.

"I'll take it," I said. But I don't plan on being anything other than mini enthusiastic about it.

plan rachel

Betty had once said about Rachel's father, "I have no idea where he is," with a look on her face that meant, *And I could not care less.*

Pressed, Betty had added, "He looked a lot like you," which felt like a counterpunch to a jab Rachel had not even made.

Betty said there were no whys, there were just things that happened, like rain and stomachaches, and kids who were born with Down syndrome, and bad vibes on the beach. She insisted they should not feel sorry for themselves.

After the fiasco with the shells, Rachel opened her laptop and ran another search for her father. She did this sometimes when she was lonely or bored or angry with Betty. Just typing his name into the search bar felt like an act of defiance.

He would certainly be "Leary," but he could be "Robert Leary" or "Bob Leary" or "Rob Leary" or even "Bobby Leary," although Betty also said he went by "Sledge." Why?

"It made him sound tough," Betty had said.

"Was he?" Rachel had asked.

"Not enough."

Maybe the name didn't fit. But on Facebook and Google and even LinkedIn (which seemed the remotest possibility), she tried "Sledge Leary" too.

She made a few assumptions—some firm, like his age, "around forty, forty-one now," Betty suggested; some reasonable, that he would be likely to live where it was warm ("he hated the cold") and that he worked with his hands; and some gut guesses, such as a home hundreds of miles from Sea Town and that he probably hadn't aged well. She looked for worn faces, smiles that seemed a little forced. His looking like her didn't seem especially helpful. Brown eyes, brown hair, a nose interrupted with a bit of a bump as it sloped down. That could be anybody. And Betty insisted she didn't have any pictures.

"What about from the wedding?"

"Burned them," Betty had said matter-of-factly—as if, of course, what else could she do?

Rachel imagined the fire in the rusting grill behind their bungalow, saw the pictures curling in the flames, the progress of the fire crawling from the outer edges in. She couldn't decide whether Betty had been drunk, buzzed, or sober, but she could picture the lighter fluid in one hand and the match in the other—a balance of forces with her mother in the middle. It would have been night, and the firelight would have danced on her face.

There was a Robert Leary on Cape Hatteras, North Carolina. He had a rusty tan and a cockeyed grin and a way of looking into the camera as if it were a familiar and almost beloved enemy.

But he was in insurance and had been for over a decade. Neither fact fit—the field or its duration. The Robert Leary she was looking for wouldn't be in anything for the long run.

Bob Leary, Santa Barbara, California. He liked local wines, selling antiques, and his committed relationship—with a man named Reggie. With antiques, there was a hustle behind all the rosewood and chipped porcelain that fit the idea Rachel had of her father. Gay did not. She suspected her father wouldn't own it, even if it were true.

Rob Leary in the Florida Keys wore a Hawaiian shirt open to his navel, displaying a carpet of gray chest hair. In his beard and his fish-stained safari shorts, he looked like a cross between Ernest Hemingway and a rumrunner—too good to be true. He was a retired fund manager who liked to keep in touch with his classmates from Yale.

There were Learys all over the country, up and down both coasts, in patches throughout the middle and southwest, and plenty across the border in Canada's bigger cities. There was even a Sledge Leary, but he was an action hero in an amateur artist's comic panels, buried deep on a cosplay site that was half swords-and-leather, half soft-core porn. This Sledge had fists of steel and a heart of gold and, for comic relief, made mashed potatoes with his fingers. Although the hero wasn't helpful, Rachel liked this Sledge and bookmarked the site.

"What's the point?" Betty had warned. "He won't take you. You'd just be deadweight to him."

But that's what Learys do, Rachel thought. Carry deadweight. She looked around her room. Shells, toys, *PowerPuff Girls* posters—there was still too much of Curtis everywhere, hanging around. Guests who wouldn't take a hint and leave.

"If you were going to college in September," Mrs. K said, "you wouldn't need a Plan Betty or a Plan Leary or anyone else's plan." For an old woman not much taller than a corner mailbox, she had a big voice with a lot of muscle, like a soft hand with a surprisingly strong grip. Stretching over the coffee table, she passed a novelty serving dish—the Campbell Soup Kids—stacked with homemade sugar cookies. "You'd have Plan Rachel," she said.

Mrs. K's cookies were too sweet for Rachel's taste, but she took one out of politeness and ate it slowly so that she wouldn't be invited to have another. Mrs. K had made a fresh pot of hot tea, which Rachel loved, and for her money, Mrs. K's sofa was the best. It swallowed her when she sat down, pillowing her on both sides with comfort. The bungalow smelled of mentholated arthritis cream and cinnamon-scented candles.

"I'm not ready," Rachel said between nibbles.

"So you say," Mrs. K said, but she didn't push. It was an old argument, and neither of them was up for it. Instead, Mrs. K sighed. With the rise and fall of her breath, Mrs. K's cotton housedress rustled like a bush shaken by a landing of small birds. Rachel marveled at her arms, sinewy, long, with skin the color of old piano keys. For the longest time, she had been Curtis's friend, not Rachel's, but Rachel had inherited her, and Mrs. K did not seem to mind, although it was obvious to Rachel, from the sweet treats that were her brother's favorite, that Mrs. K still missed him very much.

"Give me some sugar," Mrs. K used to say, surrounding the boy with her arms when Rachel brought him around. She was willing, even eager, to take Curtis for an hour or two when Rachel was at wit's end and needed a break. Over checkers, cookies, and

TV, the two of them were thick as thieves, their brows nearly touching in their private conspiracy of affection. Almost all the smaller objects in Mrs. K's house, from tissue boxes to the television remote, were wrapped in cozies Mrs. K had knit herself. Returning to pick up Curtis, Rachel half expected to find him snug, head to toe, in a cozy knit just for him. At Curtis's wake, all his old friends—and many of them really were old—had lined the walls, casting shy glances at the casket. Mrs. K wasn't among them. Her absence had touched Rachel more than anyone else's presence.

"I don't want to rush into college," Rachel said. "I want some time to find out what I want. You know, find myself."

"College is just the place for that," Mrs. K said.

"Did you go?"

"Didn't have the opportunity."

Rachel sipped her tea, looking for something to rest her eyes on other than Mrs. K. She found the cat clock on the wall, keeping time with its tail and the goggling back and forth of its eyes. Without meaning to, Rachel nodded her head in time with the clock. She caught herself and held up her cup. "Great tea," she said.

"How's your mother?" asked Mrs. K. Her gaze never moved from Rachel.

"Same old, same old."

"Is that good?"

"Good enough," Rachel said quickly. Mrs. K didn't reply. When the silence grew too uncomfortable, Rachel asked, "Do you know why anyone might be nicknamed Sledge?"

"You know someone named Sledge?"

"I might."

"Sounds like someone to keep at arm's length."

"That's easy," Rachel said. Crystals of sugar stuck to her lips. She reached for them with the back of her hand. Mrs. K, stretching again over the table, passed a paper napkin.

"Thanks."

Mrs. K returned to her seat, the cushions sighing for her. "You need company your age," she said. "I'm an old pain in the ass. And your mother has her own stuff to work out. You need friends."

"What would I say to them?"

"Whatever you want."

Rachel wasn't so sure. In high school, she had felt like a perpetual exchange student—always at the edge of conversations she pretended not to understand. Translating her terms to theirs and vice versa seemed too much trouble.

"You need to get out more."

"I am out," Rachel said, admiring the cozies around her. "I'm as out as out can be."

In the logic of amusement parks, someone had thought it clever to paint the ticket booth walls in a pattern of stones, and over its window, construct a lattice of iron bars, as if the booth were a dungeon prison—punishment for Pirate's Playground pirates who didn't play nice. The booth, little larger than a refrigerator carton and nearly as flimsy, could hold only one person at a time, and most people did not like being that one person behind the bars.

Rachel didn't mind. After Betty and Mrs. K, it was something of a relief, even if the patrons were sometimes odd or difficult.

"Fifty tickets," the customer at her window said, fishing a credit card from her purse. Two pink grandchildren stared up at the booth, one at either side of the woman. She dressed far too young for her age—fringed T-shirt and cut-off jean shorts—as if fifty-five were a rumor about someone else.

Rachel processed the card and produced the tickets without speaking, eager to keep conversation to a minimum. It was still early in her shift, daylight, and she felt achy all over from staying up late searching the Web for Learys. She worked in a hangover fog, even though no drinking had been involved. It didn't seem fair.

"How many should I get?" the next customer asked, surrounded by a restless group of kids, a cloud of noise and motion. Rachel wondered if the woman had to handle them all by herself. Were other adults waiting for her in the park? Or had they abandoned her, with the kids, to enjoy a few hours of peace on the beach?

"Get the Big Book," Rachel said. "One hundred fifty tickets." The Big Book was a hundred dollars, a nice round figure. Even though Rachel was hardly concerned about the park's bottom line, she liked selling them. She found something satisfying about passing over the Big Book, about keying one hundred dollars into the register.

"Why?" the woman asked, hesitating.

Rachel took in all the kids, fingers in noses, punches on shoulders—hands everywhere they shouldn't be. "It'll keep them busy," she said. "All day."

She made the sale. After a few more—to a young couple with a toddler, and a handful of tweeners who had won permission to roam the boardwalk on their own—the stream of customers turned into an intermittent trickle. The little air conditioner set in the wall wheezed asthmatically; being in the booth when business was slow was like sharing a hospital room with a dying patient.

Rachel had the job because Bobby Stone had made a surprise appearance at Curtis's wake. A big man who could make any room feel crowded, he'd made the funeral home airless. When he approached Betty and Rachel on the receiving line, the low whispering of the room dropped even lower. All eyes turned to him, and because he was next to her, those same eyes fell on Rachel as well. She had a vague sense of having disappointed everyone, that she had not kneeled quite long enough or shed enough tears. In fact, her eyes were dry. Everyone else's were wet.

Even Stone's eyes were damp. In a voice louder than it needed to be, given how close he was, he had said something about wanting to do all that he could to help in this difficult time. Betty, her face buried in a hand clustered with tissues, nodded graciously but said nothing.

It had occurred to Rachel that without Curtis, she would have a lot of free time on her hands. "A job," she had said.

And Stone had said "of course" with a slack smile. Only later did Rachel consider that hers was a face he would not be eager to see every day. But when spring rolled around, she realized he wouldn't have to.

"It's the ticket booth or nothing," an elderly woman with a white sweater shawled around her shoulders said when Rachel had turned in her application. In exchange, Rachel got a badge, an employee handbook, and two blue polo shirts stitched with the Pirate's Playground logo: a grinning bear with a scimitar clenched between its gleaming teeth.

Rachel yawned. She filled the dead time by bringing order to the shelf under the counter, stacking the tickets, sorting out the maps and brochures. She read and reread the employee manual. She gazed through her bars at her little square of Pirate's Playground: the entrance gate, the back end of Blackbeard's Boat. Few people walked by. Rachel felt sleepy, as if lullabied by waves she could neither see nor hear. Then a glint of light caught her attention. She blinked, refocused. At the entrance gate, a boy in mirrored sunglasses stood face-to-face with the park's mascot pirate as if absorbed in conversation. He looked left and right, over his shoulder and behind the pirate, then lifted his hand to the pirate's chest. Rachel almost looked away, the moment was so private and strange. She felt embarrassed for the boy but also fascinated: what was this peculiar intimacy about?

At the end of her shift, the good feeling of being freed from the booth was compromised by the clinginess of the late-afternoon air. Much of the boardwalk crowd had scattered for dinner and aloe vera and petty family arguments in rented condos. Rachel stopped by the pirate that had held the sunglassed boy's interest. She inspected his chest. On his billowy white shirt, in block letters carefully printed in red ink, there was a fresh violation: *Don't fall.*

June 6, 2013

Nothing like "free" to drag in the bottom-feeders.
Walter stopped at the ticket office after his shift at
Happy World to angle for a few passes. He'd never come
out and say so. Instead, he just happened to be
dropping by. He asked about the Rock-It Roll-It Coaster,
but he was hopelessly obvious.

I shook my head to discourage the confidence he
imposed on me anyway. He leaned into me and whispered
that I was right, the restraining sensor is messed up.
Sometimes it says they aren't locked when they really
are.

And the other way around, I told him.

Walter sliced his hand through the air as if chopping
off a snake's head. "No way," he said. "We've looked
into it. Not happening."

I made a crack about Stone's certified team of
qualified professionals. Did they know? Did Stone?

He looked at me as if I were an idiot. "What do you think? You can't cut the cheese in his parks without him knowing about it."

Or score free tickets, I reminded him.

Walter put on his "who me?" routine and pouted. He had cousins coming in from Philly—have mercy.

I reached under the counter and pulled out a stack of complimentary passes. I told him to use them before four or after ten. If they came when there was a crowd, Mike would give me shit.

Walter thumbed through the tickets and said Mike wasn't like that—he was one of us. We all look out for each other, right?

I'm not sure I share the sentiment. Too often, watching someone's back means looking away from something else.

"Why?" I said. "Is there something to see?"

Walter stuffed the tickets in his pants pocket. "Man," he said, "there's always something to see."

careful with tools

Chuck Waters spent so much time on the living room sofa, stretched across its length, bare feet drooping over one end, his head cradled in his hands on the other, that even when he rose to pee or grab something to eat, the cushion dents marked his spot, a crushed echo of his presence. He didn't leave the sofa often. He didn't need to. There was a flat-screen television to watch, a coffee table crowded with necessities: the television remote, his cell phone charger, a Swiss Army knife he idly toyed with as he watched CNN, opening and closing knife blades, scissors, file, saw, magnifying glass—tools gleaming with the potential to do something useful.

See? he seemed to say, although he spoke as infrequently as he moved. *It's all under control. Everything's within reach.* Ethan took a seat on the edge of the coffee table.

Chuck shook his head in disapproval. "Off the table. You know what your mother would say."

"She's not here."

"Doesn't matter." But he didn't put up a fight.

"I was on the boardwalk," Ethan said.

"Still in one piece?"

A running gag. It had been jogging and wheezing since Chuck had been fired by Bobby Stone late last September. Without his sharp eye and attentive care—without the vigilance and dedication he had applied as Stone's lieutenant—the boardwalk would crumble into timbers and wash out to sea.

It was only a matter of time.

Ethan looked at the television without really watching it. Earlier in the morning, he had spied on his graffiti to see how people would respond, and he had made a few observations: that the "double take" is entirely an invention of the movies, which no one makes in real life, ever; that if the grand plan is to see responses to your message, writing that message on the inside of bathroom stall doors is probably a bad idea; that in general the overall machinery of the boardwalk moves swiftly. Within twenty-four hours, most of his marks were already gone, either scrubbed clean or painted over. The Pirate's Playground pirate must have posed a special challenge, however; he and his upraised boarding ax had been lifted from his spot, leaving his two rumpled boots in place with screaming-red traffic cones front and back to prevent guests from tripping over them. It was odd. If you're going to carry off the pirate, why not take the boots as well?

His father would find it funny, this thing about the pirate and the boots.

"Left behind?" Mr. Waters asked quietly, as if interrogating himself. "Classic." He sighed, sat upright, and grabbed a short stack of graham crackers from a box on the table. "That'll give us confidence in the park's maintenance. It sends a message."

Another running gag: Stone and his messages. His exhortations that employees conduct themselves with care, because everything they did "sent a message." There were many things about the adult world that confused Ethan, and this "message" thing was one of them. The idea of doing or not doing a thing, not for its own good, but for some kind of message it might send, felt twisted, perverse. To be an adult was to be perpetually shadowed by your own ghost, the one sending messages.

"That's not the only thing," Ethan said, trying to shoo the ghosts away with words. "There's the Sizzleator." Ethan took advantage of an open spot at the end of the sofa. An empty space, like a missing voice in a vocal trio, remained between himself and his father. Mr. Waters looked at the television, and Ethan looked at his dad, his scrabbly, unshaven face, the electric shocks of uncombed hair falling over his brow.

"Ah," Mr. Waters said. "Walter's kingdom. Finally, after all these years, he's worked his way up to the Sizzleator."

Ethan coughed up a modest laugh. He wanted to be on his father's side, and in a way, it was funny, Walter in charge of something. But in another way, it wasn't. There was something brittle in his father's eyes, small olive pits of bitterness.

"There's graffiti on the front of it," Ethan said.

"Front of what?"

"Front of the Sizzleator. Just under the counter."

"Huh."

"In magic marker. Red. Really bright. Can't miss it."

"He'll paint over it," Mr. Waters said, "eventually. But will he use primer first? Probably not. Nope."

Ethan wanted his father to ask what the graffiti said, and he didn't want to have to ask him if he wanted to know. "From the boardwalk, it's hard to miss."

Voices from the television only amplified the silence. Ethan picked up the Swiss Army knife from the coffee table and pried open the pen knife blade. He wondered why a blade so squat and stubby was called a "pen knife."

"It sends a message," Ethan said.

"What?"

"The graffiti on the Sizzleator. 'Don't fall.' That's what it says."

More noise from the television. Two men on parallel screens but in different rooms were arguing alone into their respective cameras.

"Huh."

"What do you think it means?"

"What means?"

With the edge of the blade perpendicular to his thumb, Ethan tested the blade against his nail. It was something he had seen people do when they wanted to know how sharp a knife was. "Don't fall," he said.

"Jesus, Ethan," Chuck said, swiping the knife from Ethan's hands. "It's a tool, not a toy." He smacked it on the table with a decisive thunk.

"What do you think it means?"

Chuck rolled on his back, facing the ceiling. "If it's supposed to be advice," he said, "I don't think it's very helpful."

"You know what I don't get?" Ethan said, speaking toward the television. "Jason hated the ocean, hated the beach. What was he doing out on a jetty?"

"Ethan—"

"You ever see him in the water? Or even close? It doesn't make sense."

"Make sense?" Chuck had slung a forearm over his eyes, as if blocking an intense sun or averting a gory, horror-movie climax. "Of course it doesn't make sense. Jason was smart, but he was still a kid, and kids his age do senseless things. I did. You will. And that night, Jason did too."

"I just don't see it," Ethan said.

"That's the problem," said Chuck. "We don't want to look."

At seven, Ethan took his daily call from his mother. He could hear sirens and car horns in the background, the roar and drift-off of passing motors. "How's New York?" he asked.

"I'm sitting on a fire escape," she said. There was something girlish in her voice, as if she were leaning into a circle of girlfriends. *A fire escape! Can you imagine? Just like the movies.* "How are you?"

"Same as yesterday." When he wasn't on the phone with her, he was buzzing with a million things to say, all of them jostling for attention. Now, he couldn't think of one.

"How is your father?" she asked, the "is" drawn out like the buzz of a ripsaw. "How *is* he?"

Ethan shrugged into the phone. "Okay."

"Has he found work?"

"Some," Ethan said. Then, "None. He's waiting for Stone."

Ethan could practically hear his mother roll her eyes. "Nothing changes," she said.

"When are you coming home?" She'd left in March. Three months and counting. And Ethan counted.

"Ethan . . ."

"Just asking."

"Remember what Dr. Rogers said?"

Lowering his head, Ethan shielded himself from the coming lecture.

"About making assumptions? The vicious cycle? First you make assumptions, then you make poor choices based on those assumptions?" Ethan didn't need to see her to know she was making a circling motion with her hands, pedaling the air on a fire escape in New York City.

"And poor choices lead to stupid actions," Ethan said.

"Dr. Rogers wouldn't say 'stupid,' would he?"

"Irresponsible. Irresponsible actions lead to destructive consequences. . . ."

"Which in turn . . . ?"

"Inspire false assumptions," said Ethan.

"You're making progress."

"When are you coming home?"

"Oh, Ethan."

Any other place, it would have been ridiculous to hope for a job this late in the season. But the Sizzleator was known for high turnover. It was even something of an insider's joke, a badge of Sea Town authenticity, to work at the Sizzleator at least once for a month or two, for as long as you could stand the heat and the grease, the burns on your arms, the stupidity of its management. Even though everyone knew how miserable it was, there was an air of inevitability about the Sizzleator. It had become the place to go when you applied too late for anything better or missed a shift once too often somewhere else and lost what you had. For Ethan, it looked like a passage, a place he could enter as one kind of person then leave as someone different—if nothing else, as a veteran of a common experience.

"I don't know that I need anybody," Walter said, wiping the counter with a dirty dishrag. It was almost eleven o'clock at night, close to closing time.

"Maybe not right now—" Ethan said.

"Maybe not you," said Walter.

A year ago, things would have been very different. But that was a year ago. Before Chuck Waters took the fall for the accident on the roller coaster. Before Jason fell in the ocean.

Ethan pointed to the graffiti under the counter, the only place it had survived on the boardwalk. "You're going to have to take care of this."

"I know my business."

"You'll need primer. Two coats."

"Listen, Little Waters." Walter leaned across the counter. "This is my place. It may not be much, but it's mine."

"I know where Stone keeps stuff," Ethan said. "Paints. Rollers." He looked up at Walter. "T-shirts. Aprons."

"I got all the stuff I need."

You think so? Ethan thought. He wondered what leverage he might have as Chuck Waters's son. What would he know that Walter would not? Probably that the job others envied, caretaker to a world of amusements, was much more tedious than they would expect, much less about rides, cotton candy, and pinball machines, and more about glowing computer screens, about blank spots on spreadsheets that demanded to be filled. Then it occurred to him: "What about the numbers?" he asked triumphantly.

The double take may have been a work of Hollywood fiction,

but the craning of the neck, the turning sideways of the head left and right, the eyes sweeping the landscape for witnesses, that was real. Or at least it was for Walter. Jason had always said Walter was a clown.

"Bullshit," Walter said. "You can't mess with the spreadsheets. Even your father can't. Not now."

"We don't have to," Ethan said. "I can tell you what to put in. And what not to put down."

"Bullshit," Walter said again. But much more softly, more a caress than a curse. He looked intently at some point in the middle distance, as if watching a slide show of the possibilities: reports of inventory purchases higher than their true costs, records of sales lower than true revenues. In between these two poles of what really was and what was written down, there gleamed the promise of easy cash just asking to be taken. "You're completely full of shit," said Walter.

Ethan smiled: he had just gained entry to the Sizzleator.

Stone himself stopped in today and dropped a bomb in our laps: his daughter would now be manager of the Moon Walk Mini Golf. He drew us together in a huddle, Mike alert, Eugene following the speech over the rim of his glasses, and Amy as mute and still as a Buddha, erecting a force field of indifference around her. This daughter was conspicuously absent, and Stone, hands on hips, spoke forcefully in a way that was both blunt and vague. "You're going to see changes," he said, but for the rest of us, gazing at the ground between our feet, there wasn't anything specific to focus on, just big talk of "change," "leadership," and a new satellite in the Stone universe, "flexibility."

I give Mike credit; when Stone pulled him aside to give him the new marching orders, he had the balls to hold his ground—at least for a while. I was just within earshot, tinkering with the lunar lander at the eighth hole. When it works right, a ramp painted to look like a ladder briefly touches the ground, inviting the putt up and through the lander itself. It moves slowly, but it's still one of the trickier holes.

Naturally, the ramp jams all the time—in an obscene position suggesting a passionate desire for the ninth hole. Inside the lander, there's a cogged rotor that lifts and drops the ramp. On really hot days, the casing swells just enough to bind the cog drive. Then I have to go in and free it up. The long-term solution is a better-machined housing. But we don't get long-term solutions. We get me, on my hands and knees, dicking around with a greasy cog.

With my head up the lander's behind, I don't think Mike or Stone saw me. Mike said something about fairness, about a deal being a deal. He had put in three summers at the Moon Walk, and by tradition, if not by rights, he was in line to be manager. It was never a formal thing, just something commonly understood: you pay your dues, you get ahead. That's the way it's always worked. Mostly.

"Things change," Stone said to him. "Leadership means flexibility. . . ."

I squatted on my haunches, the rotor in my hand, wondering what would happen next. I could see the two of them square off through a portal in the lander—I'm sure Buzz Aldrin had a much better view. Mike squared his shoulders as manfully as he could while Stone let his belly speak for him—an occupier of considerable space that could not be easily moved. Would Mike storm out? Would Stone throw him out?

In the end, Stone made the first move out the door, leaving Mike to mumble something about "what goes around, comes around."

Later, in the bathroom, while I was digging grease out from under my fingernails, Mike cornered me by the sinks and vented his frustration, bitching about his "three fucking years." He appealed to the unspoken rules of boardwalk seniority that applied, he insisted, even to the boss's kids. He spat into a sink. "Where the hell has she been for the last three years?"

I rolled my head toward the open window and told him to lower his voice. The ticket office was just a few yards away. Stone's daughter stood in the middle of it, in frame and design a completely different animal from her father: a grasslands fawn to his backwoods bear, with damp brown eyes and long blond hair like curtains around her head. She kept her hands fixed at her side, as if afraid anything she touched would break in her hands. We Waterses have been working for the Stones for years, live in the same town, go to the same schools, but I can't say I know her from Adam. Or Eve.

Mike played it tough, saying he didn't give a shit if she could hear. But his voice was softer. He splashed water on his face, wiping it off with our brown, rough-and-ready paper towels. He said it wasn't fair; he deserved better.

I was right—I heard a cough, a polite clearing of the

throat, a few yards away. I was sure she could hear everything.

Don't we all, I told him. Join the club.

He made an ugly laugh. "That's easy for you to say. You're on the inside."

The inside? I didn't like where he was going. Was he talking to me or sending a message to her? "The inside of what?" I asked him.

Mike lifted his hands in the air as if balancing the world on his palms. "All of this," he said. "The whole Sea Town thing."

What, because of my dad? Because I'm a Waters? "Funny thing," I said, toweling off my hands, "I'm right here. Same as you."

"It's not the same," Mike said, leaving the bathroom. "Not even close."

green ribbon of freedom

A dark blue uniform has a way of standing out in an amusement park, a stab of midnight in the thoughtless sparkles of fun. It was late in Rachel's day shift, and there was no line at the booth; when she saw her approach, Rachel's first thought was for her pockets. Anything incriminating in there? Any nail polish that might squeal, any perfumes that could rat? But the red cones where the pirate had been spirited away restored her good sense. This was probably about the *Don't fall* graffiti. She rehearsed a description of the vandal in her head, his short stature, his mirrored aviator glasses. Justice, she thought with satisfaction, was about to arrive.

The officer was of medium height, fit, with a slab of blond hair bound behind her and the permanent squint of someone who spent her life in the sun; without the uniform, she could have been a surf princess or one of the day-boat operators who ruled the bay piers as if they were old family estates. "Rachel Leary?" she asked.

"Yes," Rachel said, surprised to be addressed by name. But the police had probably been poking around, asking who might have seen something. You would expect that.

But she did not expect a request to accompany the officer to the station.

Involuntarily, Rachel looked up, for advice from people who were not there. "The station?"

"We have a few questions."

"Don't I need some kind of permission or a lawyer or something like that?"

A thin smile. "It's not like you're under arrest or anything," the officer said. "Your shift ends at five thirty, right?"

Without meaning to, Rachel put her hands on her pockets, patting the reassuring nothing that was in there.

The police station was a sullen, eggshell-colored box as broad and flat as an open hand. Police cars and ambulances hived in its sunbaked lot; a couple of officers, furtive as schoolboys, smoked cigarettes around the corner from the front door. Rachel's officer acknowledged them with a nod. Inside, she exchanged a few words with a colleague at the reception desk, a thick-faced man who, after registering Rachel's presence with a lizard's slow glance, showed no further interest in her. Beyond him, a handful of desks, loaded with outdated computers, were manned by officers in short-sleeved blue uniforms.

"Come with me," Rachel's cop said, leading her between the desks to a glass door striped with blinds at the back of the office. It opened into a small, dim room with one long table and two people, a man and a woman in civilian clothes, who clipped their conversation short when Rachel entered and dismissed Rachel's officer—she had come to think of her as her own—with a curt thank-you.

"Miss," the woman said, waving her to a chair, "we hope you can help us by answering a few questions." The badge on her blouse simply said, CLEMMONS. Her mule-brown hair was cut military short, and she had a small mole above her lip that, on a prettier woman, might have been attractive. Betty, Rachel thought, would know what to do with this woman. Rachel almost felt sorry for her. "Detective Ryan and I just need a little more information before we can officially close our case," Clemmons said.

Detective Ryan nodded in sympathy with his colleague's statement, his hands clasped together over a yellow legal pad. He had a scrubby black mustache and heavy jowls that gave his face a look of perpetual falling, as if life and gravity had collaborated to drag his face down. His eyes, wet and red, seemed irritated by allergies or exhaustion; they rested on Rachel without energy or focus. A ballpoint pen, tucked between his intertwined fingers, aimed at Rachel's heart. "This shouldn't have to take long," he said with some exasperation, hinting that it was out of his hands. No, if it were up to him, this unpleasant business would be over fast. But it wasn't up to him, he wanted her to know. When he lifted his elbow from the manila folder under his arm, Rachel could read the neatly printed label: LEARY, CURTIS.

"This is isn't about the graffiti?" Rachel asked.

"You can clarify a few things," Ryan said, splaying the file open. "I hope you can help us. That you'll speak freely."

Detective Clemmons smiled wanly at Rachel, as if to say, *Yes, you can. You have what it takes. Help us, won't you?* Rachel couldn't find it within herself to smile back. Wasn't Curtis's case already closed? What was left to say that hadn't been said before? She felt a cool breeze on the back of her neck. A faded green ribbon, filthy with dust, fluttered from the grill of an air vent. *Why do they tie ribbons to vents?* Rachel wondered. *Do people really feel cooler when they can see the air is blowing?* "This is about the accident?" she asked, the question catching in her throat.

"We're just straightening out some details," Ryan said.

"Like I explained in the hospital," Rachel said, "I didn't actually see . . . what happened." In her first interview, just hours after the accident, Rachel had spat out fragments of answers between sobs, between spasms in her chest, her muscles heaving as if abandoning her bones. Out of mercy, officers sat sandwiched at her sides to steady her. In the hospital, Rachel remembered, the air was meat-locker cold.

Rachel gazed down at the table, lingering on its scars: penned scribblings, small starbursts of scratches. Her hands had formed fists on their own. *How dare they?* Rachel thought. *Without my permission.* She made her fingers relax.

"We know," Clemmons said. "That's all right."

"Why am I here, then?" Rachel asked. "Have you found something new?"

Nothing changed in Ryan's hangdog expression. "You were watching Curtis that day," the man said, flipping through papers in the file. "Did you do that a lot?" he asked.

"Do what?"

"Watch your brother. Was that something you had done before?"

"All the time."

The detectives exchanged glances, sharing an understanding

concealed from Rachel. Clemmons picked up the questioning. "Was there anything unusual that day?" she asked.

"Well, yeah," Rachel said. "It's not every day your brother dies on a roller coaster."

More shared glances. "Before that," Ryan said calmly, crossing his arms over the file. "Anything out of the ordinary?" When Rachel didn't reply immediately, he generously offered her a minute or two to think about it. "We'd rather have a complete answer than a quick one."

Facing these detectives was like walking on the jetties at night, Rachel thought. One misstep, one slip on the bladderwort that covered every dark rock, and you could wedge your foot between the stones. The tide could roll in over ankle, knee, and higher, but try as you might, there was no climbing out. Whether or not such a thing had ever really happened, its possibility was part of the local lore everyone knew yet no one really respected. The threat didn't keep drunken teenagers from wandering out on the rocks, but it did give them fear or bravado or both. Now Rachel just felt anxious.

She went over the day in her head: Betty getting ready for work, Rachel struggling to get Curtis out the door. Her stomach hurt, and she was irritable; she had thrown up twice the night before and suspected there would be more to come. She needed a break, but Curtis was Curtis. For him, pulling on his shorts was a game; putting on a shirt was a game. The more frustrated Rachel became, the more satisfying the play—for Curtis. Ordinarily, experience provided wisdom, inspiring patience. But whether it was the hour, her stomach, or the usual conflict with Betty—who always needed something, a mirror, her tube of apricot scrub, an opinion on which of two blouses would best match her pants and flatter her eyes, all this while Rachel was neck-deep in Curtis care—wisdom and patience had kept their distance.

She'd been rough with Curtis. Rachel hadn't remembered that part of the day before, lost as it was in the accident that clouded everything preceding it. She had been rough buckling his belt into place. She had been rough bending his arms into shirtsleeves. Rough getting him out the door, rough towing him toward the boardwalk.

When they got there, Curtis wanted to go shelling, saying, "C'mon, c'mon," as if they'd all be gone if he didn't hurry, eager to gather his fill before anyone else beat him to it. There was never any competition, but he couldn't imagine a world that didn't love what he loved as greedily as he did. He would race around the beach, gathering shells into the fold of his shirt before anyone had a chance to deny him his treasure. "No playing on the rocks," Rachel had told him. "Stay near the high-tide line."

"The tide line?"

She pointed it out to him—a ragged trail of seaweed and beach litter that marked the farthest reach of the water. He nodded his head as if he were listening—which wasn't likely—and darted down the stairs and through the gap between the dunes. By standing over the rail, she could see him poking about, bending and scooping, holding his finds up to his eyes, stuffing things into his jacket pockets that met his approval, indignantly discarding the things that did not.

Rachel's attention wandered. She was digging her nails into her palms to distract herself from the queasy feeling inside when she felt a sharp tug on her pants. "I found a new one," Curtis, suddenly at her side, said gleefully. He reached inside his pockets, his tongue in the corner of his mouth, and pulled out a mud-colored shard about as thick and wide as a potato skin, but with sharp white points, like tiny peaks of meringue, along two of its edges. It looked like the breastplate to a miniature suit of armor.

"You found a crab shell," Rachel said. She didn't care to touch it—trash, a carcass carrying a whiff of its innards. Nausea rallied inside her.

"Uh-huh, a shell."

Rachel took a deep breath, preparing for battle. "It's not a real shell. Well, it's a shell, but a different kind of shell."

"But it's a shell," Curtis insisted.

"It's an animal's shell," she said. "The kind of shells we collect, they come from shellfish, like clams and mussels."

"Aren't they animals?"

"Yes, but they're not shell animals, like what we think of when we think of shells or collect shells. What you have there is the cover of a dead animal. See? It once had legs and claws and eyes. . . ."

Curtis looked closely at the crab shell, turning it over in both hands. "Where?"

"They're not here anymore," Rachel said. "The crab died. The claws broke off. All that's left is this shell."

"So it's a shell!" Curtis said happily.

Rachel gave in with a sigh, finding it easier to quit than to keep fighting. "You're right. It is."

"Yours," Curtis said, holding it up for her. "It's for you."

Rachel remembered taking it between the tips of her fingers, thinking of the gulls that had pecked the flesh out, the runny guts in the sand, the casual violence romanticized as "nature."

"Thanks," she had said, determined to throw it back on the beach or into a trash barrel when he wasn't looking.

The detectives looked at Rachel expectantly. All this time, she had been gazing at her hands, fixating on a scar that remained from a cut she got just hours after the accident when midway through an argument with Betty about who should have been watching whom, she had thrust her hand into her sweatshirt, ripping her palm across the jagged shell. It was a bloody mess, more casual violence, and her first real opportunity to cry freely that day. It had felt good to let the tears flow, let the argument fall aside, let Betty clean and bandage her hand—to simply let go for a few moments and be Betty's baby for a minute. They had both welcomed the break.

"It was just like any other day," Rachel finally said. "Nothing special."

Ryan leaned back in his chair, which scraped hostilely against the floor. "Did you see anyone you knew, any friends?"

"I don't think so."

"You sure?"

"How about at the food court?" asked Clemmons. She drew the folder to herself, turning over a few pages. "I'm sure it's not easy to remember everything."

What was she expected to remember? Rachel wondered. The food court? She had wanted a cup of tea and had hoped to pacify Curtis with an ice cream cone. But just when she thought she had him—and a moment's peace—Curtis had to go to the bathroom. And not just any bathroom, not the one just yards away at the back of the court, but the one by Happy World. There had been a little scene when Curtis raised his voice to get his way, clutching his pants at the crotch and shouting that he had to pee.

Rachel knew better—Curtis was being manipulative, standard-issue behavior she dealt with every day. But, just as Curtis had anticipated, he had attracted attention. And as Rachel had come to expect, outsiders saw a boy with Down syndrome who merited their sympathy, not a shrewd player who knew how to get his way. Someone had talked to these detectives, sharing something "important" that they happened to remember, which in the aftermath of a big event, just happened to give them a momentary sense of self-importance.

"Lots of people knew Curtis," Rachel said. "By sight, I mean."

"Curtis kept you on your toes," Clemmons said helpfully. "I'm sure he could be quite a handful. I'm sure it wasn't always easy looking after him. That's a lot of responsibility. Especially for a young girl."

Rachel shrugged. Curtis wasn't the only person who could be manipulative. "He wasn't so bad," she said.

"Tell us more about the Ferris wheel," Ryan said.

"What about it?"

"Didn't you go on it?" he asked. "What happened when you did?"

Rachel looked from one detective to the other. "I think you already have some idea."

"We're filling in the blanks," Clemmons said.

"You know," Rachel said, thinking of the blanks in the story she'd rather not fill, "I'm only eighteen. Shouldn't my mother be here with me?"

Ryan tilted his head toward a black phone on the table. "We could do that. It's certainly within your rights. But," he said, leaning forward over the table, "eighteen is the legal age of consent. And we thought you might want to speak more freely."

There was that word again, Rachel thought, *freely*. The more she heard it, the less she felt it.

"Maybe," Clemmons added, hands clasped primly over the file, "there are things you need to say that you don't want your mother to hear."

"I can't think of any," Rachel said.

"About the ride on the Ferris wheel?" Ryan prompted, lifting his eyebrows, the most animation there had been on his face yet. "Wasn't he . . . restless?"

"What do you mean?"

"Did he have trouble keeping still?" Ryan thumbed through a few pages in his pad, holding the pen in his teeth the way a pirate boarding a captured ship might hold a cutlass. He took the pen out again and waved it over his notes. "You said in the hospital that he had been a handful that day, that you needed to get him out of the house."

Rachel nodded.

"You rode together on the Ferris wheel?"

"Yes."

Ryan looked from his notes, drilling his red eyes on Rachel. "At some point, he tried to stand up?"

As if on cue, the air vent's green ribbon fell limp and still. Even though it was impossible for the room to change temperature so fast, Rachel felt hotter. She thought, *This ribbon thing really works*. "I see where this is going," Rachel said. "You want me to say it was my fault. That I should've known better."

Officer Clemmons seized Rachel's hand with both of her own. "This is so difficult," she said. "We know."

The enclosing grasp felt confining. Rachel pulled her hand free.

"We have an eyewitness who said Curtis made an attempt to stand up while riding on the Ferris wheel and that you pulled him back down again," Ryan said.

"Someone could see that from the ground?"

"Is it true?" Clemmons asked, leaning back in her chair. "Look, this isn't about placing blame. This is about understanding what happened. Did he try to stand up on the Ferris wheel?"

"I don't remember," Rachel said. She put a tissue up to her eyes, not because she was crying, but because she wanted to cover them. And she wanted to buy some sympathy. Manipulation seemed to be the order of the day.

"Let's move on to the roller coaster," Ryan said. "The attendant checked his height?"

"Yes."

"When he got in the car, Curtis sat down without trouble?"

"Yes. He'd been on the ride before. He knew what to do."

"Would he have stayed down, all the way through the ride?"

"Why wouldn't he?" Rachel asked, looking from one detective to the other. Ryan averted his face, finding renewed interest in his pad, his notes. But Officer Clemmons held her gaze without blinking; she seemed to have shed all her softness, exposing granite in her eyes.

"He had a history," Clemmons said.

In a flash, Rachel imagined outrageous attempts at escape, wild actions with broken glass and gunfire, reckless behavior that people would later describe, shaking their heads, as "so unlike her, so unlike her." There would be random shouts. Running figures. An all-points alarm to capture the fugitive girl flying out the door. But the impulse passed as quickly as it had arrived, and Rachel was almost surprised to find herself still seated at the table, still facing two detectives.

"He didn't stand up," she said hotly. "He may have been retarded, but he wasn't stupid."

Ryan whispered something to Clemmons, and Clemmons nodded. The green ribbon began to flutter again, and Rachel thought, *Good, it will be cooler in here soon.*

"Well," Clemmons said. "I think we have all we need."

"Really?" Rachel said. "Did you talk to that attendant? What about the other ride—what do you call them—operators? What about Stone?"

Ryan closed the file. "You can be sure that we talked to everyone that matters," he said.

Impossible, thought Rachel. *You couldn't talk to Curtis, who matters most, because he's dead. You talked to the sister who was watching him that day, and you wondered, What person in her right mind would let a disabled kid get on a roller coaster after pulling him into his seat on the Ferris wheel? What kind of person would do that?*

"Thank you," Clemmons said, rising from the table. "We have everything we need now."

What kind of person?

Ryan cleared his throat. "You can go now," he said. "You're free to go."

What kind?

"Miss? Miss Leary?"

"What?"

"You're free."

June 30, 2013

We call her the "fairy tale princess" and keep as far away from her as we can. Maybe it's the distance, but from our perspective, it's hard to believe she's Stone's kid. When she asks you to do something, it's like an apology. "Would you sweep the greens? Can you check the restrooms?" No one wants her to be bossy, but for reasons I can't explain, her mousy little voice and question-mark commands make me angry. Just tell me what to do, and I'll do it—but don't ask for my consent.

We all feel that Mike got a raw deal, and we show our loyalty to him by maintaining a conspicuous silence around the princess. We're hardly subtle. When she's near, conversation stops. As soon as she steps away, the whispers—loud whispers—begin.

Mike pushes it further, hiding keys, crashing the computer, letting in friends for free during peak hours. Diana—the princess—either doesn't notice or doesn't want to notice. The more she pretends to ignore him, the more Mike pushes, as if he's daring her to take it all the way and fire him. "Screw it," Mike said to me. "What do I have to lose?" He won't quit, and the princess won't call him out. The tension around Diana rises every day.

Even Walter feels it. "What the hell's going on?" he said when I handed him his tickets—I didn't bother to wait for him to ask this time.

I told him it was the Mike thing. Stone's daughter taking over.

Walter shook his head and said that was tough, but that was the way of things. He said I should know.

I said I knew.

Then Walter changed the subject, drawing himself up to tell me that he got a new job with new responsibilities.

I said nothing. He seemed frustrated by my lack of curiosity.

"Pirate's Playground," he said. "I'm a supervisor now."

How was this possible? My father must be thrilled. I know I'm not. Me—Moon Walk toadie. Walter—supervisor. "Really?" I asked.

"Really." Walter practically floated with glee. Whatever disappointment he may have had with my previous indifference had been more than made up by the look of surprise I couldn't hide on my face. "Really," he said, stuffing the tickets in his front pants pocket. "Really, really."

It wouldn't be the last surprise. Yesterday the princess pulled me aside. This time, I braced myself. She pointed out that our fathers work together.

Together? I said my father worked for her father.

"That's what I mean," she said. "I mean, you know what it's like—to be the boss's kid."

"My dad's not the boss."

"He's in charge of people, a lot of people. He may not be the boss, but he's a boss."

Yeah. And that's why I have this terrific job here.

She wanted to know why everyone was so . . . so . . . and wasn't able to complete the question. She asked me if it was about Mike.

It isn't and it is, I thought. It isn't, because there are so many little injustices with root causes we can't see that we focus relentlessly on those we can. It is, because Mike may not be someone we love, but his getting screwed is something we understand. It isn't, because in another week or so no one will give a shit about him. It is, because the fairy tale princess who has no right to our submission will get it anyway. Is it about Mike? I nodded and said nothing.

"I didn't have anything to do with it," she said, brushing her hair away from her eyes. "It wasn't my idea." She looked around as if she was taking stock. "Does anyone really think I'd want to be . . . be . . ."

"Hated?"

"Yes," she said, biting her lip. "Who'd want that?"

I told her it didn't matter. In the end, she was the manager, and he wasn't.

"I get it," she said. "I just wish it didn't have to be so fucking weird around here."

Just over her shoulder, I could see Mike leaning on a broom handle, giving us the evil eye. I looked away. "How could it be anything but weird?" I asked her.

Then today, I was sorting the clubs by size when Mike nudged me in the ribs. He lifted his chin to the ticket office. Stone was inside, talking to his princess. "That bitch is going to rat us out," Mike said.

"For what?"

"For anything. For the thing with the keys. For missing clubs." Mike looked me in the eye. "For giving away tickets."

I said I wasn't so sure. I'd seen park guys slacking off, but it hadn't occurred to me to run to my dad. I learned a long time ago to mind my own business. At least when it comes to people. Point me to a ride, and I'll poke around, but people have a way of poking back. Yet I doubted my own doubt and wondered if Mike might be on to something.

Diana's hair tends to cross her face when she leans over the register to ring up customers. It was crossing her face now. We couldn't hear what she was saying, but Stone came in loud and clear—his is the one voice that can be heard above all others on the boardwalk, no matter how crowded it is.

The word "tickets" came up, and Mike gave me an I-told-you-so expression. I pulled out a screwdriver and moved in closer to the office, pretending to fuss with a light fixture tucked about knee-high in the hedges.

Frankly, it gave me a way to get away from Mike too. He was getting on my nerves.

"Where'd they go?" Stone asked. "How can you be short by almost forty tickets and not know about it?"

I could just barely hear her. "I don't know," she said. "I screwed up the numbers."

"You screwed up the numbers?" He paused, challenging her to fill in the silence. "This isn't about math. This is about staff. Your people."

"I don't think so."

Stone lowered his voice—just a little. "Diana, they're testing you. Don't you see that?"

"Everything's fine," she said. "I just lost count of a few tickets."

"You didn't lose count of anything."

"I'll make up for it. Out of my own pay."

Whatever self-control Stone had, he lost it. His hand came down hard on the countertop, rattling a cup of pencil stubs. "How can anyone respect you if you don't respect yourself?" It was too harsh, even by his own standards. His voice softened. "You can do this," he said. "I know it's in you." When she didn't respond, he made a sigh that sounded familiar—I had heard it often enough from my own father. Stone turned and left.

Mike sidled up next to me. "You hear that?" he whispered.

"That's Stone," I said.

"Not him, Diana. Listen." He held up his hand, crossing-guard style. "She's crying," he said gleefully.

It was true. Though her hair shielded much of her

face, her shoulders were shaking and her breath jerked irregularly. She probably was crying.

"Boo hoo," Mike said.

I drove my screwdriver into the ground. I told him to fuck off. Didn't he have any real work to do?

chapter six

a christmas present

The Christmas tree lay on its side at the foot of the basement stairs as if it had tripped on the way down and then died there from neglect. In fact, it hadn't budged since the day in February when, in an unusual display of emotion, Chuck Waters had bear-hugged the tree and lifted it, stand and all, without regard for the string of lights that was still plugged into the wall or the ornaments that scattered around his feet as he carried it to the basement door and heaved it angel first into the gloom below.

"There," he had said, presumably to Ethan's mother, although she had gone upstairs a half hour before, "the tree's down. Happy?"

Now it was June, the edge of the first summer since Jason's death, and Ethan stood at the top of the basement staircase, peering into the darkness, burning with indignation. He hadn't thrown the tree down, but he was going to pick it up. His father had not been pleased when he learned that Ethan had found a job at the Sizzleator, found it without asking, without discussing it, without drawing upon Chuck Waters's knowledge of, and contacts on, the boardwalk. "You just walked up and asked for a job, just like that?" Chuck had asked.

"Yeah," Ethan had said. "More or less."

"The rules have changed," Chuck said. "At least out there." That was when he got the idea that the basement really needed to be straightened up and Ethan would be the right man to do it.

"Why now?" Ethan had asked his mother during their daily call. He thought she would back him up, have a few words with his father, insist on being fair.

But all she said was, "It's long overdue."

Finally, something they can agree on, Ethan thought bitterly. What was it they had been fighting about before she went upstairs? Before his father got up from the kitchen table and crossed the television without so much as a glance at Ethan? Before he strode to the Christmas tree and, after a brief pause eyeball-to-eyeball with a crystal Santa, thrust his arms through the branches, strangled the trunk, and lifted the tree from the floor?

There were times, Ethan understood, when it was best not to ask questions; they coincided with the times he most wanted to ask them. His father's throwing the tree down the stairs was one of them.

This he did remember: that it was long after Christmas, even after Valentine's Day—there were already Easter decorations in the stores. Now, standing at the door to the basement looking down, fighting back questions about the point of all this and its injustice—questions that would only make his work harder and longer—Ethan allowed his eyes to adjust. Downstairs, one bare bulb fought a losing battle against the darkness surrounding it.

For reasons Ethan couldn't begin to fathom, his father refused to put anything greater than forty watts in the light socket. He drew a deep breath through his nose, testing the cool air, the musty smell of mildewed tent canvas, rusting iron tools, and abandoned seedbeds.

Straddling the Christmas tree, Ethan began unwinding the light strings, wrapping them around his palm and elbow the way he had seen his father's crew wind up extension cords at Happy World. He set the coils aside and retrieved empty boxes for the ornaments. Ethan tucked the ones that had survived the fall carefully into their boxes. After removing all the ornaments he could see, he rolled the tree, like a patient in a hospital bed, to reach the ones underneath. Shards of broken ornaments glittered on the rough basement floor, as if the tree had bled broken glass.

Ethan disassembled the tree, folding the limbs against the trunk, straitjacketing the wiry arms of coarse plastic needles. Before, this had been a joint effort of "the boys," and doing it together had blunted the melancholy of the season's end, the three of them fussing and joking over what belonged where, who had which box, and how on earth everything would fit back into the boxes. Jason was the most methodical of the three and had an almost preternatural gift for packing each box like a three-dimensional jigsaw puzzle, the newspaper-wrapped ornaments nestled together without gaps. Meticulous work Mr. Waters greatly admired.

When they carried the boxes downstairs, Mr. Waters would get distracted by all the reminders of unfinished business that had found their way downstairs: the blender he had planned to fix, the flower boxes he was going to paint and install under the street-facing windows. Ethan, who rarely went into the basement, treated it as an opportunity to explore the unfamiliar. Poking through boxes and bench tools, he caught hell from both his father and brother, who would bark him away from the boiler valves and demand that he put down the reciprocating saw he held aloft like a madman chasing teens through the woods.

But being in the basement by himself did not give Ethan a welcome sense of freedom. Instead, he felt a last-man-standing kind of anxiety, a lonely apprehension that there would be no one remaining above when he had completed his work below. He tried to shake off the feeling and concentrate on the tree, placing each part in the tall, narrow box that, when his father carried it upstairs, had always formally announced the beginning of the Christmas season in the Waters home.

In keeping with his father's instructions, Ethan stacked the ornament boxes in the far corner of the basement opposite the oil tank; they stood precariously, like an old man with a bit of a stoop. He steadied the large Christmas tree box on an overturned milk crate that would keep the tree above water should the basement flood. It never had, but neighbors on either side of the Waterses had gotten wet basements after unusually rainy springs. Dad had seen the pump hoses rolled out of their basement windows and then made it a rule to put anything important at least a foot above the basement floor. "Planning ahead," he had said, "is what saves you in a disaster."

The coils of lights came next. "On the emergency shelves," his father had said. On the east side of the basement, he had knocked together some scrap lumber from work to build a wide set of shelves that held items the family might need in an emergency—a hurricane, a winter storm, or an overloaded electric grid that had simply collapsed from exhaustion. Many of the provisions made sense—canned soups and raviolis, bottled water, a first-aid kit, a twelve-pack of toilet paper—but others seemed odd: What would they do with the bottle of hair gel on the shelf? Why the cans of frosting or the disposable razors? And the baseball bat—the last line of defense against unnamed what, zombies? Ethan picked it up, testing its heft. He made a few low, loose swings, semaphoring the bat by his knees. He pictured rising waters that might stream by his ankles then rise up his legs, the bat useless in his hands. He wondered, would it float? If Jason had found a bat like this bobbing in the water, would it have been something to cling to? Or just another thing he'd have brought down with him?

After clearing the tree, Ethan scanned the floor for strays. Broken ornaments had left a sheen of silver that twinkled as Ethan moved around the basement searching for survivors. There were fragments everywhere, under the shelves, against the staircase footings, even under the oil tank.

With a few minutes of stooping and pecking, Ethan—an anti-Santa—had gathered most of the largest pieces into a white trash bag. Just as he was about to twist up his bag, he saw a glint under the oil tank. Reluctantly, he lay on his stomach and looked underneath. A plastic angel was just within reach, and he grabbed it, but that wasn't what gleamed. He probed farther, touching a flat edge he thought must be the wall. But it couldn't be; it had an edge, a corner, beyond which a silver ornament shaped like a tear-drop remained outside Ethan's grasp, even when he shifted himself parallel to the tank to shoulder under it. To Ethan's surprise, there was much more space behind the tank than it appeared.

He got to his feet, brushed the dirt from his shirt, and approached the tank by its narrow side; a stack of boxes concealed the gap. He disassembled the stack from the top, careful not to trigger a cascade tumbling down on himself. Pulling aside the top box, the head, exposed nothing but black air. But after the second box, Ethan saw a chrome clamp light, like a photographer's flood lamp, clipped to the rafters. Strange. With greater curiosity, he removed the third box and faced a steel folding chair. The last box on the floor he brushed aside with his foot.

Ethan's heart raced, as if he had just stumbled upon the evidence of an interrogation meant to remain secret. It was like the set to a scene that looped through his head ("You'll never make me talk." "Oh, we'll make you talk, all right!"), but it was real and just feet in front of him. Although he knew there was no one nearby, Ethan turned around, listening for footsteps, movement, the hard breathing of someone watching intently. The kitchen refrigerator hummed overhead. An acoustic guitar whispered from a neighbor's radio. Again, the last-man feeling came over him—everyone above had been sucked into the sky by aliens or angels. Or they might as well have been.

Ethan reached for the clamp light, feeling for the switch. He turned it on, then blinked in the sudden brightness. The light revealed a cord that ran through the floor joists toward an outlet elsewhere in the basement. *Why go to the trouble?* Ethan wondered. He kneeled on the chair and looked behind it. On the floor was a low, black trunk bandaged with peeling bumper stickers. Scarred metal knuckles reinforced the corners; on one broad side of the trunk, a leather strap hung loosely, like a large dog's panting tongue.

Ethan gripped the chair back, bracing himself against a weightless feeling threatening to push him over. The trunk had to be Jason's. The idea was less a thought than a sudden gut conviction. Reason followed the feeling in a progress as calm and measured as a principal's footsteps. His mother hated the basement—she said it gave her "the willies" and refused to enter it. If she needed something from downstairs, she always sent Jason to get it. For his father, the oil tank space would've been both cramped and unnecessary—the basement was already his; he wouldn't need a private fortress within it.

No, this was the kind of place a boy might retreat to. And in the trunk? Whatever Jason wanted to keep to himself. Like what? Dope? Love poems? Dirty magazines? Plans for world conquest? Ethan folded the chair, which screeched as it collapsed on itself, and leaned it against the wall.

There was just enough room to swing the trunk lid open. On top, he found a box of Cheez-It crackers (against his better judgment he nibbled one and spat it out: stale) and an opaque plastic pouch that looked promising—rare coins, knives, pills?—but only held pens, pencils, a draftsman's compass, and a thick pink eraser. Beneath these were stacks of comic books and a few magazines: sequences of Green Lantern and Spider-Man, a two-year-old *Scientific American* and a couple of *Popular Mechanics*. Farther down, Ethan found some papers, school papers, exams crawling with elaborate equations and figures. Teacher praise, of the kind Ethan rarely saw himself, shouted in red pencil. "You show much promise," said one note, canted diagonally on the margins of the page. This, Ethan marveled, Jason found not just worthy of keeping, but of hiding. Isn't that what makes treasure treasure? Burying it?

More school papers. More magazines. Nothing interesting. But from within the snug space between the trunk's side and the magazine stack, Ethan withdrew a marbled notebook, one of the cheap kind, piled high at the five-and-ten at the end of every summer, which no one ever brought to school anymore. Ethan slipped it out of the trunk. The corners were scuffed down to the cardboard; the spine had been reinforced with strips of silver duct tape. He opened it carefully, as if the pages would turn to dust and dissolve between his fingers. Inside, he saw page after page of precise handwriting that was exceptionally easy to read, unlike his own. Here, behind an oil tank under the incriminating glare of a clamp light, he scanned pages with dates, pages with places he recognized, pages with people he remembered. Then, when Ethan found it the first time, he knew what he had been looking for all along, bobbing within the waves of words: his name.

Before leaving the hiding space and restoring the boxes in the gap between wall and tank, Ethan retrieved the silver teardrop from behind the trunk, placing it gently on top of the lid. The journal, he carried with him.

July 9, 2013

Drinking on the beach always sounds better than it really is. Mike organized "a little something" for the crew at the Moon Walk, and in a gesture that said he was ready to move on, he made sure to invite the fairy tale princess.

I think she thought it was a good idea too, a way to show that she was just one of the gang. Things started well: Mike passed along some cold ones from a cooler he had hidden in the dunes. I'm not big on the beach—I almost never go in the water—but I can see the attraction. Many nights, the wind whipping off the ocean is so strong it takes the breath out of your mouth. But last night, the breeze was easy, invitational.

It's strange how a feeling can be shared in a crowd, and at first the softness of the night was reflected in a kind of unspoken goodwill. After two beers, everyone lightened up—it was as if we were all grateful that the tensions of the last couple of weeks were beginning to dissolve.

Eugene, Amy, and Tango pulled some wood out of the trash—driftwood, broken recliners, umbrella poles—and with the aid of some beer case cardboard, they managed to get a fire going. We sat cross-legged around it and kept an eye out for cops, though they usually don't bother with the south end of the island. Tango pantomimed his adventures in last year's hurricane surf, showing us what it was like to get beat up by real waves. Eugene made himself custodian of the beers, opening them for everyone, and Amy, who has more tattoos than bare skin, dropped her imposing goth scowl and actually looked, well, sweet in the firelight. For a while, it was kind of magic—all of us together, having a corny beach moment that for once was real. If I had a girlfriend, this would have been the moment to draw her closer, my arm around her waist, her head on my shoulder. But I didn't, and I felt so good I didn't mind so much. For a while, the mood was mellow.

But it couldn't last. With the third and fourth beers, the joking leaned a little harder. "I'm Tango," Mike called out, tossing his head back luxuriantly, plumping invisible dreadlocks on his shoulders. In the firelight, a crowd of eyes, like those of wild animals crouching in the midnight woods, shifted to Mike, then Tango, then Mike again. Even with the surf in the background, you could hear the fire pop. Otherwise, there was the loaded silence of people holding their breath.

Tango broke it with an awkward laugh. Now that

they had permission, voices surged forward like wedding-party drunks joining a conga line. Eugene did a passable version of me lecturing about gear ratios. "It's all about torque," he said, squinting his eyes and making a lewd grab at his crotch. Mike got something of a comeuppance from Tango. Tango twisted his face in a snarl, sneered at the sea, and said, "Fuck the water, man. What's the ocean ever done for me?"

Even Diana got in the game. "I'm Amy," she said, rolling her eyes in exaggerated contempt. It was the least elaborate mocking so far, but it drew the biggest laughs. Amy, perhaps numbed by her beers, didn't respond with the comeback we expected. Ordinarily, we were all a bit intimidated by Amy, what with her tattoos and her dark sarcasm. She could sting, but now she looked a little pale and wobbly. We sensed an opening and within seconds, there was a pile on: Tango laid into Amy about her "sore knees," and Mike made a knowing reference to a club in Longport and some goings-on behind the back door. Amy played the good sport, smiling—but her eyes went begging for shelter. The evening was cracking up. I got to my feet, brushing the sand from the back of my legs.

Mike blocked me with his bottle. He grinned and asked me where I thought I was going. I could see the flames gleaming off his teeth.

I said it was time to pack it in. There were a few murmurs of agreement.

"Already?" His voice carried an I-don't-think-you're-going-anywhere tone. "It's early, and besides, it's your turn." Mike waved his bottle before the rest of the crowd. "What do you think, everybody? I don't think it's right, Jason leaving before he's had a turn."

"Ah, let it go," Tango said, driving his heel into the sand.

"Wouldn't be right. We have democracy, a participatory democracy." Mike took a swig from his beer. "There are rules of fair play. At least out here."

No one missed the reference, Diana least of all. She turned away from their eyes, gazing at a far spot on the wet horizon.

Amy, relieved by the shift in attention, asked who was left.

"Jason to do one. And Diana," Mike said, pointing at her with his bottle, "to be done. No one's done Diana yet."

Eugene encouraged him. "C'mon. Let's see you do Diana."

I said I didn't think so.

"Christ, just do it and get it over with," Tango said.

"Yeah," Amy said. "Just do it."

"All right," I said. They were all watching me now, and I could feel a kind of heat coming from their eyes—the wolves leering from the underbrush. My hair had blown over my own eyes, and I reached up to brush it aside.

"Ha!" Mike said.

For a moment, I was confused because I hadn't even started, hadn't even thought about how I would "do"

Diana, when I realized I already had without even thinking about it. That thing with the hair.

I saw a few faint smiles in the firelight.

"Umm," I said softly, "could you see if there's tee pee in the restroom and, you know, restock it if, you know, there isn't enough?"

Amy snickered, rocking backward and forward in the sand. I felt a growing confidence.

"Guys," I said, wringing my hands together, "could you look around for lost balls? I think we're missing some balls."

"Oh, man," Tango said. Eugene shook his head in mock disapproval. Mike carried the largest smile, a triumphal arch turned upside down on his face.

I was feeling my beers, their approval, and something more obscure I couldn't name. "We're getting low on balls. Won't someone help me find them? Please, someone, help me find my balls."

Laughter. Rich but not generous, full of bile and teeth. A crowd of rocking bodies around the fire, hands circling the throats of their bottles.

"Good one," Diana said flatly when the laughter trailed away. She said she considered herself done. Attention shifted her way, all at once and all together—from many parts, one mind.

"It's just a game," I said feebly.

Diana raised her hand: stop. She got to her feet. Maybe it was a trick of the light or the way she was illuminated against the sea, but she looked tall or at least taller than I had estimated. "Good night," she said toward the fire. "I've got to get up early. Look for lost balls."

They laughed less hungrily this time, and as Diana disappeared behind the dunes, the party spirit left with her. I stayed and finished my beer.

island of misfit toys

A shadow crossed the book in Rachel's lap. She looked up from her reading. The barred window seemed filled with a single grin, a mouthful of large yellow teeth rimmed with plump watermelon-pink lips. The eyes, like those of Mrs. K's cat clock, could not keep still.

"Yes?" Rachel asked, hoping her voice might startle the face away. She pushed her book onto a shelf and closed her knees.

"We're going on the rides," the man said, his hands fluttering up to his shoulders like startled birds. He looked like an oversize boy who had gotten lost and strayed into his mid-thirties; there were creases around his eyes, black licorice strands of hair fell limp over a balding brow. Behind him, a well-rehearsed voice from another man told him to tell the young lady what he wanted. Sitting up, Rachel saw an elderly couple standing behind the grin at the window, their postures molded in patience.

"Tickets!" the man said triumphantly. The couple smiled— two thin and similar smiles fully prepared to wait.

How many times had Rachel been in their shoes? Too many to count. "How many would you like?" Rachel asked, directing the question at the guardians.

But the woman, instead of appreciating Rachel's understanding, clasped her hands stoically below her waist. "That's for him to say."

Okay, Rachel thought, sighing. She knew this game: empower the disabled. She'd been there, done that—but from the other side of the glass. Now it was only just that she cooperate.

"Well," Rachel said, "we have single tickets for one dollar each, thirty for twenty-five dollars, fifty for forty and"—she was reluctant to say it, anticipating what would come next—"the Big Book."

"The Big Book!" The man, as Rachel had expected, liked the sound of that. His head rocked back and forth in delight.

The old man stepped forward, making a breach in the back line. Alarm rang in his eyes. "What's the Big Book?"

"One hundred fifty tickets for one hundred dollars."

"Oh," said the woman. "We certainly don't need that many. Roger, you don't need one hundred fifty tickets."

It was too late. "The Big Book! The Big Book!" Roger shouted. His spit rained against the glass.

"Roger—"

"The Big Book!"

"So," Rachel said, crossing her arms. She had tried to avoid this, but they had cast aside her better judgment. "What'll it be?"

"That's up to Roger," the woman said, a lifetime of resignation in her voice.

"Big Book!"

It had been almost a year, but it was like riding a bicycle,

Rachel thought—there are some skills you just don't forget. Tickets? Well, fifty tickets come in a nice little booklet too. She slid one under the window and winked at the parents. "Here you go," she said. "The Big Book."

The old man reached for them first, the back of his hand mapped with blue, earthworm veins. He presented the booklet to his wife, the two of them thumbing the deck of tickets, then they engaged in a silent conference of glances. Rachel expected one or the other to produce cash or a credit card, but instead she got a dark look, ominous as a storm cloud, from the mother. "Is this the Big Book?" she asked.

"Sure," Rachel said, still playing the game.

The woman slapped the packet on the counter. "I don't believe it is," she said. "Roger asked for the Big Book. We will take the Big Book." Her husband mirrored her iron look and nodded his head in agreement.

All this time, Roger stayed at the window, his hands still fussing at the air around him, but it wasn't likely he remembered why he was there.

"I just thought . . . ," Rachel began, then stopped. It didn't matter. She swapped ticket packets, pushing the Big Book under the glass. "One hundred dollars," she said.

The old man produced a credit card. "A nice round number," he said, smiling.

Rachel tried to smile back. "Yes," she said. "It is."

"Say thank you to the nice young lady," the mother said.

The words struggled out of Roger's mouth, shy and short. "Thank you," he said, spinning away, a parent now at either arm.

"You're welcome." Rachel watched them walk away and waited for it, the slip of his hand into his mother's. She had forgotten it—that little thing that came after everything, the slip of one hand inside another—but it came back, this memory, a bit haggard after a long trip away, yet determined, insisting on its rightful place beside her.

What? Rachel asked the memory, the ghost hand seeking warmth in hers. *What do you want from me?*

It was a little after six o'clock, the sun still ruled the sky, and Happy World was every bit as unbusy as the Playground. Rachel would not admit it to herself, but she had expected an empty space of air and asphalt where the roller coaster stood as solid and rooted to the earth as an old oak tree. There was no yellow police tape or barricade of hastily assembled plywood panels, not even a stabbed-together cross of wood with flowers leaning against it, the kind of impromptu memorial people compose at traffic accident sites. There was just the Rock-It Roll-It Coaster, a glittering tangle of rails under a hot and unforgiving sun.

Yet there were changes. Instead of a single ride attendant, there were now two, both in red Happy World vests, both lazing back against the guardrail killing time before the crowds came. And on an enameled panel leading up to the loading ramp, Rachel found a message, rough and jagged, something someone waiting impatiently on line might have scratched into the paint with a house key or a hair pin. In a sloped print stumbling downward from left to right, as if sliding off a shelf, it said, *Caution, falling children.*

The attendants talked quietly to each other. One swung a set of keys from a black lanyard. The other was making a case for the Phillies, arguing that this could be a playoff year. The key swinger seemed unimpressed. When Rachel approached, they both straightened up.

"I'm looking for someone who operates this ride," she said. "A black guy, but light-skinned. Real thin."

"What's his name?" the key swinger asked.

"I don't know."

"How many black guys work here?" the Phillies fan asked. "It's got to be Leonard. You mean Leonard?" He pillowed an aura of empty space around his head. "Crazy hair?"

"Yeah, that's him." That was pretty much all she remembered. Skinny black guy with a lot of hair. Otherwise, a blur. Rachel didn't think it was much to go on, but she suspected it would be enough. There just weren't that many black kids employed on the boardwalk.

"He doesn't work here anymore," Key Swinger said. He drew the blade of his hand across his throat. "Gonzo. Out."

"Did he quit?" Rachel asked.

"Well," Phillies Fan said, shifting his weight and looking over Rachel's head, a seasoned ranger reading the horizon, "I believe he was highly encouraged to quit."

"Why?"

Key Swinger gave his colleague a warning look. "He's gone," he said sharply, "and that's all we know."

"That's all we can say," added Phillies Fan.

"Know where he went?"

"No."

"Does anybody else who works here know?"

"No," said Key Swinger, who turned his attention to his colleague, poking his shoulder. "We got to get back to work."

Looking left and right, Rachel confirmed that she was alone. She put her hand over her eyes, surveying a crowd that wasn't there. "Yeah," she said. "You can't keep all these good people waiting."

Phillies Fan laughed. But Key Swinger turned his back to face the controls, signaling the end of the conversation. Phillies Fan stopped laughing, then made a low and discreet wave of his fingers, like a catcher behind home plate, that pointed to a line of porta-johns under the flume ride.

Rachel played along, nodding back. As she walked toward the flume, she heard Phillies Fan ask for coverage. "I have to use the head, man."

"Make it quick," Key Swinger said. "Stone likes to see two people here."

Rachel, planting herself at the far end of the line of porta-johns, admired the attendant's caution; from where she stood, they wouldn't be seen from the coaster. She didn't have to wait long.

"About Leonard," Phillies Fan said, keeping his voice low. "Lots of us think he got a raw deal."

"What do you mean?"

Phillies Fan stuck his hands into his pants pockets. "Some shit happened, and he caught a lot of the blame. Maybe all of it."

"What happened?"

"I can't really talk about it," he said, looking over his shoulder. "Though that's all people are talking about." He jerked his head toward the roller coaster. "Last year. Toward the end of the season. A retarded kid fell off the ride. Probably got too excited and tried standing when he shouldn't have." He made a diving motion with his hand. "You hear about it?"

"No," Rachel said, looking at his feet. He wore plaid canvas high-tops. Stupid shoes, she thought. Just plain stupid.

"This town is better at keeping secrets than I thought," he said.

"You know where Leonard is?"

"Maybe," Phillies Fan said.

"Please."

Whether he was in a hurry to get back to his station or he'd just gotten bored being coy, Rachel couldn't say. But he released the information he had. "There's a go-cart place. Not the one by Pirate's Playground. Downtown. At the old train station. You know it?"

"I've passed it," Rachel said.

"I'd look there." Phillies Fan spat on the ground. "It's one of the few places Stone doesn't own."

A desert of asphalt heat, Sea Town's middle blocks sat stranded in still air, unrefreshed by the ocean breezes from the east or inland winds off the bay on the island's west side. Here were all the necessary things that made the dreamy things possible. Filling stations. Convenience stores. A fenced-in lot of squat, green transformers that seemed to groan in their beds of crushed rock.

The old train depot lay thickset and Victorian just past the electricity substation. Before Rachel saw the go-carts, she heard them, a chorus of shrill, lawn-mower whines. Above the Gothic filigree of the old station's entrance gable, a faded wooden sign said, SEASWIFT GO-CARTS. The office filled a tiny space no bigger than a closet where the ticket window once had been; the remaining space was sealed off, most of the windows covered in plywood hastily painted to match the mud-brown clapboards and trim of the station. A beetle-green bicycle leaned against the wall.

"Is Leonard here?" Rachel asked at the window. Inside, seated in a desk chair too small for his bulk, a fat teen with wire-frame glasses worked a Game Boy in his hands.

"On the track," he said without looking up.

An otherwise simple oval, the raceway was pinched in the middle to break the monotony, with an island of old tires at its center and a starting line at one side where waiting go-carts idled in the heat. Business was no busier here than at Happy World; there were only two carts on the track. One was raced by a white boy about nine or ten years old, who drove with his shoulders to the wheel and his tongue in the side of his mouth. The other driver had to be Leonard; he drove with one hand on the wheel, his elbow lounging on the side of the cart. He seemed intent on letting the boy stay just ahead of him. But when the boy turned around, Leonard put both hands to the wheel and made a show of determined effort. The boy laughed ruthlessly.

After a few more laps, the engines died, and the drivers coasted back to the starting line. Leonard stepped out first, withdrawing legs that seemed impossibly long for the tiny cart. He helped the boy get out. It looked like a familiar routine; Leonard extended his hand, and almost without looking, the boy grabbed it and let himself be pulled forward as he stepped over the cart's side.

"See you tomorrow?" Leonard asked.

"Probably," said the boy.

"C'mon," said Leonard. "Definitely."

"Probably."

"We'll see," said Leonard. He watched the boy walk to his bike, then pulled a pack of cigarettes from his shirt pocket—a

Hawaiian short-sleeve dominated by broad, ruby flowers. He replaced them when he saw Rachel. "He comes every day," he said, walking toward her. "Or at least every day I'm here." He gave Rachel an appraising look, as if she were an exotic species that had strayed beyond its natural habitat. "You want to ride?" he asked.

"No," Rachel said.

"I didn't think so," Leonard said. He pointed to his shirt pocket. "Mind?"

"Go right ahead." Leonard smelled of exhaust fumes and gasoline, not a promising context for striking a match. As he lit his cigarette, Rachel took a precautionary step back. There was something courtly about him, the air of a nineteenth-century country squire, but he couldn't have been much older than eighteen or nineteen. The dissonance puzzled her.

Leonard plopped down on a bench behind them, which, like everything else at the SeaSwift, seemed knocked together with whatever was at hand, in this case, a few painted two-by-fours on aluminum poles set into asphalt, without a back to lean upon.

"You're pale," Leonard said, pulling a drag from his cigarette. "No, wait, that's not right. The proper word is *fair*. Pardon me— you're fair."

"You had it right the first time," Rachel said, sitting down. "I'm pale."

"That don't bother you?"

"I don't like the sun."

"Cancer," Leonard said knowingly, staring down his cigarette—a schoolteacher eyeballing a mischievous pupil.

"No. I just don't like the feel of it."

"I guess you're fond of the dark?"

Rachel shrugged. "Not especially."

"Well, then," Leonard said, stretching his legs. "That puts you in a difficult spot. Until someone invents a time that isn't day or night."

A light breeze swept over the track, stirring discarded ticket stubs, and Rachel smelled gas again, even more distinctly. She shifted farther down the bench, away from Leonard and his lit cigarette.

"What's the matter?" Leonard asked.

"I think you spilled gasoline," Rachel said.

Leonard lifted a knee to his face and wrinkled his nose. "I can't even smell it anymore," he said. Then he leaned over toward Rachel and sniffed. "You smell like buttered popcorn."

She leaned away from him, surprised, an involuntary tango partner. People just didn't go around sniffing other people, breaking the invisible buffers that kept strangers strangers. But against the urge to push him away, she remembered her need to pull for information. And besides, she thought, admiring his tumult of hair, he was kind of interesting. "I was just at Happy World," she said, shifting herself upright.

"I thought you didn't care for rides."

"I don't," Rachel said.

"Thought so. You must be a true townie. You live here long enough, and you don't care about sun, surf, rides, or the rest of it. At least that's my story, and I'm sticking with it. If I never see a gull again, I'll die a happy man." He blew a stream of smoke from his nose.

A voice yelled out from the ticket office. "Hey, Leonard, whatcha doing?"

Leonard held his cigarette poised in midair, as if posing for a publicity still. "I'm attending to a customer," he said.

"I don't hear any motors running."

"She doesn't like the noise. I'm pushing her around the track."

"For God's sake. Just don't be goofing off. And don't let me catch you smoking."

"Wouldn't think of it," Leonard said, taking another drag.

"Is he the boss?" Rachel asked

"He likes to think so." Leonard shook his head, amused by his thoughts. "The Island of Misfit Toys."

"What?"

"You know. Rudolph?" Leonard pointed to his face. "With the nose so bright? Guiding Santa's sleigh? The island Rudolph visits with the elf who wants to be a dentist. Man, that's whacked. Who the hell *wants* to be a dentist, right?" He balanced his palms in the air. "Pulling teeth? Making toys? Toys win every time."

"I get Rudolph," Rachel said. "But why is this the misfit island?" *Any more than Pirate's Playground or Happy World or any other place on the boardwalk—or in Sea Town*, Rachel thought.

"Rejects," Leonard said, grinding his cigarette stub under the toe of his shoe, an ankle-high work boot stained with grease. "It's where people go when Bobby Stone doesn't want them anywhere else."

There was a rattle of glass and steel. By the ticket office, a seagull perched at the edge of a trash barrel, picking through the garbage. Leonard found a small chunk of broken asphalt and chucked it at the barrel. The clang startled the gull, who flew up with an ugly caw of protest. Leonard looked at Rachel carefully, more closely than made her comfortable. She drew her legs under her.

"You got a name?" he asked.

"Rachel."

"Just Rachel? Folks couldn't afford to give you a last name?"

"Leary. Rachel Leary."

Leonard pulled at his ear. "Leary. Leary. I'm Leonard. Leonard Washington Washington."

Rachel shook his hand, a slender hand with long fingers, like a piano player. She gave him a firm shake, because she hated a dead-fish handshake herself. He returned a firm grip.

"Well?"

"What?"

"Aren't you going to ask?"

"Ask what?"

"You meet a man named Washington Washington, and you're not curious? You don't want to know why he has the same name twice? This is something you see every day?"

"Okay," Rachel said. Despite herself, she started to smile, which felt alien to her. It had been a long time.

Leonard shook his head. "No, not okay," he said playfully, gripping the bench by the edge and gazing out over the track. "Uh-uh. You got to do better than that."

"Please," she said. "C'mon. What's the story?"

"Okay." Leonard turned to her. "But are you ready for this? There are some things you just have to be ready for."

"I'm as ready as I'll ever be."

"Fair enough. My father's name was Washington. So that's one Washington. And then my mom, she swears her family is descended from *the* Washington, you know, first president, dollar bills, cherry tree? And she just couldn't bear to leave her family out of my name. Pride. She's a proud woman. So my dad's Washington wasn't good enough. She had to add her own Washington. Or there wouldn't be any peace."

"Was there peace?"

"Wouldn't know," Leonard said, lighting another cigarette. "My daddy left before I was old enough to remember him."

While they talked, the sun steadily declined, drawing mustard streaks on the scudding clouds. "So," Leonard said, "why do I have the pleasure of meeting Rachel Leary this evening?"

"Well," Rachel said, gathering up her courage, "it's about the accident."

"What accident?"

"At Happy World. Last year."

"What makes you think I know anything about it?"

"I was there," Rachel said, "and you were there too."

There were creases on either side of Leonard's mouth. When he smiled, they gave him an angelic look. But when he stopped smiling—and he had stopped smiling—they made him look years older than he could possibly be, as if at any moment he could take off his young man mask and surprise the world with an elderly gentleman waiting underneath.

Leonard snapped the remainder of his cigarette toward the line of go-carts. "People can't stop asking me about that accident," he said. "But I'm tired of talking about it."

"I wouldn't bother you if it weren't important," Rachel said.

"Yeah? You said you were there, right?"

"I was."

"So what do you need me for? What can I tell you that you don't already know?"

"I want to know why," Rachel said.

"Then you need a priest or a philosopher or a psychic with a crystal ball, but not Leonard Washington Washington," he said, standing up and straightening out his shirt. "I think you got a picture of that boy in your head you want to get out. Well, let me tell you something. It don't come out. Talking about it won't make it go away. There aren't enough words. So don't bother."

"I can't make it go away," Rachel said. "I don't even try. That boy?"

"Yeah?"

"He was my brother."

"Jesus," Leonard said softly, the old man peering out of his eyes.

"Hey, Leonard!" The fat kid from the ticket booth was yelling again, this time leaning out the window. "We got people waiting." At the station, three enthusiastic boys pulled away from their mother, pointing to the track and making claims on the carts they wanted: the red one, the one with golden stars, the green one with yellow stripes.

"I got to go," Leonard said. "Funny thing. I live in AC. But every summer, my mom sends me to Sea Town to stay with my aunt. You know why?"

"Why?"

"Because it's safe. How funny is that?"

July 14, 2013

When I came in to open the mini golf, Tango pulled me
aside. He said Mike was gone.

I said I wasn't surprised. Considering. After the
thing at the beach, you'd have to think his days at the
Moon Walk were numbered. Frankly, I wondered about
my own.

"No," he said, pulling his dreads back behind his
neck and fixing them with a wide elastic thing striped
like a coral snake. "I don't just mean from here. I mean
gone. Disappeared. I mean Wild West, left town kind of
gone."

So what? When Mike didn't show up for work
yesterday, most of us just chalked it up to a hangover.
Rumor had it he may have been fired, but the fairy tale
princess wasn't saying—in fact, she was quieter and
paler than ever, practically translucent. Out of pity, we
were just going about our business, no hassles, no

conflict. When business was slow and the princess was alone in the ticket office, she was as still as the astronaut on the Moon Walk sign over her head. They made quite a couple, two beings whose spirits had abandoned this world for another far away, leaving their hollow bodies behind.

Tango kept going. Mike hadn't shown up for work. Mike hadn't answered his phone. Late yesterday evening, Tango dropped by his apartment. No answer. After ringing the bell and pounding the door a few times, Tango swung around the back alley to tap at his window. Enough light came in from the hallway to show that the room was empty: no bed, no belongings. Just a small pile of trash in the corner—pizza boxes, soda cans, a few rags—otherwise, the room was completely stripped bare.

"Real spooky," Tango said. He picked up a club and gave it a few one-armed swings. "I've heard about this kind of thing before but thought it was just bullshit, you know, people just talking."

Against my better judgment, I took the bait. I asked him, "What kind of thing?"

Tango looked over his shoulder to the ticket box. The princess hadn't moved an inch. He lowered his voice. "People who cross Stone have a way of . . . leaving," he said. "For good."

I told him he was right—it did sound like bullshit. Sea Town's a dry town in the shadow of Atlantic City, and here in our family-friendly little cocoon, there's a kind of admiration, almost envy, of the bigger city's glamorous, wide-open vices. They have casinos, cocktail waitresses, and Mafia dons; we have clam shacks, beach patrols, and Stone—and we like to imagine that he's more than he is. Sure, Stone can be tough. But he is hardly a tough guy. My dad's worked with Stone for nearly thirty years. If there was anything weird going on, I'd know about it. I told Tango as much.

"If anything was going on, what would your father do—write you a memo?" Tango said he hadn't believed it either, but facts were facts.

Seriously, I said, what did he think? That Stone had him whacked?

"You don't have to kill someone to get rid of them," Tango said. "Let's just say Mike was probably highly encouraged to move on."

Mike was getting ready to leave, I said. He was bitter, and he hated it here, and he made his move. Not, I thought to myself, before taking one last parting shot at the princess. With my help. "He wanted to move on," I said. "And he did."

Tango shook his head, insisting on the weight of the evidence. What about the phone? What about his friends? Would he leave without saying a word?

"Maybe he wasn't such a good friend," I said.

"Maybe," Tango said, walking away. "Maybe."

Later, the princess finally left the ticket office. In fact, she damn near scared me to death. I was locking up for the night, squaring the clubs and balls away in the bunker behind the restrooms, when she

99

came right up behind me. I must have jumped three feet in the air.

She said she had to ask me something.

After what I did to her at the beach party, I expected a demand for an apology. Then she hit me with another surprise.

"I need to find an assistant manager."

"Why?" I said, trying to make light of it. "Did you lose one?"

She let that one pass. She said it would mean better pay and more hours. "I know you're saving for school, so . . ."

That was true, but how'd she know? Dad talk to Stone, Stone talk to her? It irritated me. Then I took a deep breath and dismissed the conspiracy. Who isn't saving for school? Even so, I brushed her off, saying I wasn't interested.

Diana upped the ante: she'd handle all the paperwork; I would take care of the attractions, the facility stuff. Maintenance.

"Like my dad?"

"Sure," she said. She bit her lip. "I really need the help."

I asked her about Amy, Tango—why not one of them?

She raised an eyebrow. It was the most animation I had seen in her since the party. "Would you promote them?" she asked.

I thought for a few moments. If Mike's apartment was

really empty—and I didn't think Tango had any reason to lie about that—then he was really gone. And truth is, I could use the money. Living away from home won't be cheap.

"All right," I said. "Sure."

The princess smiled. "I'm glad," she said.

make-believe
ballroom time

Rachel woke up to stirrings in the kitchen: cabinets opening and closing, the clicking of igniting gas jets on the stove. Betty had been out late the night before, so Rachel hadn't expected her to get up first, and she was right. In the kitchen, a man in a tangerine bathrobe—Betty's—stood barefoot at the counter, a tablespoon in one hand.

"Just looking for the cereal," he said. "I didn't wake you, did I?"

Rachel said he hadn't. He was lean, rangy, with gray streaks in his dirty-blond hair. He had a trucker's tan: copper-red forearms that didn't match his paler bare legs.

"Bowls are over the sink. Cereal's over there, on the counter," Rachel said.

"Thanks."

"Milk's in the fridge."

"I might have figured," he said. "Rachel, right? I'm Dan." He shifted his spoon to his left hand and extended his right. Rachel shook it. There was a spider tattoo, a black widow, on his fore-arm. He caught her looking at it. "Got it before I knew better," he said. Grinning, he added, "I should've got a tarantula."

"Nice robe," Rachel said, taking a seat at the table.

"Yeah. Well." The kettle whistled on the stove, and Dan busied himself preparing a mug of instant coffee. "You want some?" he asked.

"I'll pass," she said. "I have to warn you, that jar of cof-fee's been here awhile." Two boyfriends ago, Rachel knew but didn't say.

"I take what I can get," said Dan. He brought a bowl and a box of shredded wheat, which he winced at, to the table. "But the milk's fresh?"

"See for yourself."

They didn't say anything else while he took his first few spoonfuls of cereal. Dan drew the folds of Betty's bathrobe around him, closing a gap at his chest that had opened when he sat down. He seemed embarrassed, and Rachel liked that. Once last winter, when Rachel had gotten up in the middle of the night to go to the bathroom, she was startled in the hallway by a man with nothing on but a towel around his waist. He wasn't at all embarrassed, and Rachel didn't like the way his eyes followed her as she slid past him sideways to reach the bathroom. Back in her bedroom, she had locked her door, then pushed her dresser against it, just in case. Fortunately, she never saw him again. And she never brought him up with Betty.

"You're what, nineteen?" Dan asked.

"Eighteen."

He repeated it softly as if testing its solidity. "Eighteen." He said he'd give anything to be her age again. He'd give his right arm. He held the arm with the spider tattoo out over the table—evidence before the court. "In a heartbeat," he said. "I'd give this to be your age again."

"I don't think it's a good deal," Rachel said.

"You don't know," Dan said. "Just wait. Wait and see."

Although she had other plans before her shift—she had wanted to find something she could take to Leonard Washington Washington, an excuse for going back to SeaSwift—Betty insisted Rachel swing by Mrs. K's to drop something off, a picture of Curtis inside a frame crusted with little seashells. Betty made no apologies or excuses for Dan, but Rachel hadn't expected any. She understood.

She didn't care to dwell on it, but there had been a boy last year, Nicky, a senior with AP classes he affected contempt for. In the six weeks they had seen each other or dated or were boyfriend-girlfriend or hooked up—no words for it really fit—Nicky imposed his dreams upon her. As in real dreams, the destination constantly shifted, like a horizon seen through a kaleidoscope. He was going to write a novel. He was going to start a band. He was going to be an environmental activist. He was going to hitchhike across the country. He was going to meditate in Tibet. He was going to paint in Brooklyn.

In the end, as college admissions rolled around in the spring, Nicky was going to Buffalo—a legacy admission of his father's.

"I like the cold," he had said to her when he got his admissions package.

"Good thing," she said. She had no admissions packages because she had made no applications.

That was the last time she had really talked to him. He always wanted to talk about where he was going, and Rachel had nothing to bring to the conversation. At first she felt awkward, then bored, then annoyed. But the whole thing made her feel very adult.

They had sex—a first for both of them. And she wasn't drunk, stoned, or in love, any of the usual excuses. After six weeks of hanging out and exchanging text messages—neither confident in what it was they were supposed to do or not do, say or not say, feel or not feel—they had raced to the finish line just to get there and be done with it. There was nothing particularly triumphant in the crossing.

When it was over, she patted his back as if comforting a baby, a gesture she had used so often with Curtis that it had come to her automatically. He had nodded, as if to say, *Okay, okay,* though what or who was okay wasn't clear. It was just okay.

And when he didn't call or text her the next day or the day after that, she felt relief. No high drama. None of the wailing she had seen other girls indulge in, producing a theater of tears and hugs just to assure themselves that something of consequence, anything, had really happened.

Rachel knew better. In the end, it was as matter-of-fact as a handshake. And when she passed Nicky in school halls, on the street, or on the boardwalk, there were few hard or awkward feelings.

That, Rachel felt, had been a reasonable kind of love.

"How thoughtful of you," Mrs. K said when she accepted the picture. "Thank you."

"Thank Betty," Rachel said. As she saw it, Mrs. K already had more than enough pictures of Curtis as it was. "Not sure where you'll fit it."

"I'll make room," Mrs. K said, holding the picture aloft with both hands. "Shells. Nice touch."

"That was Betty too."

Mrs. K nodded her head. "I'll consider it a collective effort. Speaking of which, how are things going with your fresh starts, your new beginnings?"

"We're still firming up plans," Rachel said.

"I see." Mrs. K might just as well have said, "Bullshit"—the meaning was the same. And she would've been right.

At SeaSwift Go-Carts, Rachel sat on a curb opposite the station, her backpack between her knees, waiting for closing time. Two banks of stadium lights cast a sour glow on the track. Moving crablike beside the go-carts—one hand on the wheel, one on the door frame—Leonard and two coworkers steered them into a corrugated shed behind the station.

The lights snapped shut one by one, and Rachel had to let her eyes adjust to the dark so that she wouldn't lose track of Leonard. Fortunately, he cut a distinctive silhouette: shaggy hair and long, wiry frame—the outline of a palm tree.

"Ms. Leary," he said very formally when Rachel approached.

"Mr. Washington Washington."

"You remembered?"

"Of course."

"Mr. Washington Washington doesn't like to disappoint a lady," he said, lighting a cigarette. "But I'm going to disappoint you."

"You think?"

"I know. I've had to talk to the police, and I've had to answer to Bobby Stone. I'm done. I'm not talking about the accident anymore." He spread his hands low like an umpire calling safe. "It's over."

"That's not what I'm here for," Rachel said, unzipping her backpack. "I brought you something."

"Me? What could you possibly have for me?" He laughed, but Rachel noticed that his eyes didn't move from the pack.

She lifted out a small, iridescent, green gift bag and gave it to Leonard by the handles. He picked it up by the tips of his fingers as if it were too delicate to hold.

"Open it," Rachel said.

Like a mummy, the gift was wrapped in swaths of white tissue paper. Leonard unwound it carefully, releasing a doll about the size of a cupcake. It had black slippers that curled at the toes and a pointy blue cap. In its hands was a book with *Dentistry* stitched on the cover.

"The misfit elf," Leonard said. "I'll be damned."

"I happened to be near the Island of Misfit Toys, so, you know, I swung by, picked this up. . . ."

"Thank you." He held it up to his eyes. "I'll give him a place of honor on the TV. That way I can see him from the couch." Leonard ground out his cigarette, looking absently over the go-cart track as if he were already at home, admiring his gift. "So," he said after a long pause. "What's next?"

Rachel really didn't know. She had planned just far enough to visit the least likely store on the boardwalk—a shop that sold Christmas ornaments and holiday knickknacks, of all things—and had the presence of mind to get him that elf. She felt no need to tell him *how*—a deft swipe of the hand while the saleswoman answered her cell phone. The emerald bag and white tissue paper she had pulled from an alley Dumpster. The value of the gift was in the thing itself, not the way she got it.

"Should we look for the abominable snowman?" Rachel asked lightly.

"I think it wiser to avoid him," Leonard said. "I know my limits. How about a cup of coffee? There's this place I like on the bay."

"I drink tea," Rachel said, regretting it immediately. Tea, coffee, what difference did it make?

"They might have that," Leonard said, unfazed. "No guarantees, though."

A few days ago, it had felt dangerous to sit with Leonard on the same bench; now, Rachel noticed, she was following him to his car, a weed-green Plymouth Duster with a primer-red passenger door. He opened it for her, and she resisted any hesitancy, slipping bravely inside.

"Safety first," Leonard said, indicating the seat belt over her shoulder as he got behind the wheel. He buckled himself in. "I don't really need this car. But I like having it. Sometimes I think that one day, I'll just get in it and go."

Rachel admired the hula dancer on the dashboard, poking at her straw skirt to make her hips swing side to side. "Go where?" she asked.

"Details," Leonard said with a dismissive wave of his hand. He dropped the car into gear and slung his arm over the shoulder of Rachel's seat, his head turned to back up. "It's just about the going," he continued, facing forward again. "I've thought more about the getting away than the going to. That's where I draw a blank. But I imagine freedom fills in the blank."

"I just finished high school," Rachel said. "And now all I can think about is running away."

"Running away?" Leonard laughed. "At our age, it's not running away. It's growing up. Aren't we supposed to pick up our little feet and scamper off? Somewhere?"

They had turned onto a broad avenue spiked with lagoons and their little fleets of pleasure craft. As freshly built condos gave way to older, less impressive, and far more weatherworn dwellings, Leonard slowed down, then eased the car to the curb. If Rachel hadn't been directed to the coffee shop, she would never have known it was there. There was no sign on the door, which was squeezed between a bait shop and the harbormaster's office in a cramped row of shingled buildings on creosote piers jutting out, like teeth, into the bay. A small bell jingled as they entered. Inside, a ceiling rail of stuttering fluorescent tubes cast a pallid light on a counter studded with salt and pepper shakers and ketchup bottles. At the far end of the place, just past a row of red vinyl stools, a pair of sliding glass doors opened onto a few feet of dock and the iron-black waters of the bay. Now and then a boat would rumble by, sweeping a ray of light ahead of its bow.

"We'll sit at the counter," Leonard said. "I like to have my space."

He wouldn't have to fight for it. At the end of the counter, an elderly man dressed improbably in a dark suit and tie huddled over his coffee mug. Two florid middle-aged men in sun-faded cotton work shirts sat at a small table that seemed to rest on their ample bellies. They shared a newspaper between them and said little, exchanging the kind of shorthand that couples understand after years of marriage. The last remaining person was the cook behind the counter, a square-shouldered black man of about forty with a red bandanna tied over his head. Without prompting, he brought Leonard a mug of coffee and a cinnamon bun on a sheet of wax paper. "Miss?" he asked Rachel.

"Tea, please," she said. "With milk."

"Do we have that?" the cook asked himself. He poked among a few boxes on a shelf over the grill. "I got Lipton. You drink Lipton?"

Rachel would have preferred Red Rose, with freshly boiled water poured directly over the bag and steeped for exactly three minutes, then served with a touch of whole milk and just one teaspoon of sugar. The cook brought her a cup of hot water with a tea bag slouching on the saucer. The label looked faded, like an old lace doily, as if it had been exposed to years of morning sunlight. Rachel drowned the bag in the hot water, submerging it with her spoon until it stopped struggling to come to the surface again. "Thank you," she said.

On a ledge above the coffee urn, a radio played big band music that was hardly louder than the hissing gas jets under the grill. "Come here a lot?" Rachel asked Leonard.

"Yup," Leonard said. "Just about every night."

"For a guy who just wants to hit the road and go," Rachel said, surveying the counter, "this seems like a pretty got-up-and-went kind of place."

"I think of it as welcoming. Don't know if you noticed, but there aren't that many black folk on this island."

The cook had his back turned to them, scraping the grill, but he chuckled as Leonard spoke.

"How'd you find it?" Rachel asked.

"I don't know. I was walking around one night and saw a light on and people going in, and I wondered, what is this? And being curious and all, I went in. The rest is history."

The radio welcomed listeners to *Make-Believe Ballroom Time*, encouraging them to find partners and dance. "If you can't find a partner, close your eyes and invent one. After all, it's *Make-Believe Ballroom Time*."

"It's like a speakeasy," Leonard said. "Except"—he lowered his voice—"most of the people who come here at night have stopped drinking." He looked around. "It's a bar for ex-drunks. A bar without the booze."

"For fishermen too," said the cook, refilling Leonard's mug. "For fishermen without the fish." He turned to Rachel. "Another Lipton?"

"You mind, Stan?" Leonard said. "I know there's no real privacy here, but do you have to break the spell?"

Stan held up his hands in protest. "Forgive me, brother. Just refilling your coffee."

"I'll let you know if I need more coffee."

Stan gave Leonard a half-cocked smile, then retreated to the far end of the counter, where he exchanged a few softly spoken words with the suited man. Rachel nursed her tea, turning down a bite of Leonard's cinnamon bun. Everything was hushed until the twilight mood was broken by a passing boat that swung its bow light through the doors, illuminating the coffee shop in a sudden glare like a policeman's searchlight. At once, every head turned toward the light, expectant. Then the boat, and the moment, passed.

"Tell me about the accident," Rachel said.

"We were having a nice night."

"You didn't bring me here not to talk," Rachel said. "They say he tried to stand up. Tried to get out. What do you say?"

"It shouldn't have mattered," Leonard said.

"What do you mean?"

"The restraining bar in his lap. You ever go on the coaster? There's a bar right on top of your—well, right on you. You just try to stand up. Try to wiggle, even." He lit a cigarette. "Just try."

"No smoking," Stan said without looking up.

"What, you got eyes at the back of your head?"

"No smoking. It's the law."

Leonard rolled his eyes. "You mind?" he asked, reaching for the saucer under Rachel's cup. She pushed it toward him, and he stubbed out his cigarette. "What a waste," he said.

"So you're saying he couldn't stand up?" Rachel asked.

"I'm saying the bar should've stopped him. And I'll say to you what I've said to everyone else. To the police. To Stone. I checked those bars." His voice grew softer but more insistent. "They were down. Before that ride began, I checked every car. Up and down. Like we're supposed to."

"And?"

"And they were down. Tight. There's a fail-safe too, on the controls. If all the bars aren't locked, you get a red light. And the coaster won't start. I had a green light." He looked out toward the bay. "Like starboard, right? Out there, on the water, green is starboard? Red is port, I think. You sail?"

"No. So what happened?"

"You know what happened."

"I mean, how did it happen?"

"Don't know," Leonard said. He held up his mug. "Stan."

"You know the magic words," Stan said.

"Please? May I have more coffee?"

"Certainly," Stan said, pushing himself away from the counter.

"All I know," Leonard said, "is that they say it's my fault." After the accident, he was brought into a little room at the police station and asked a lot of questions. "Actually, the same questions, lots of times," said Leonard. They took his blood for a drug test, and they took down his words. "It would be crazy to say that the police work for Stone. Nuts. Paranoid." Leonard waved his fingers in the air. "But let's just say that their interests are—what's the word?—*aligned*. They gave me an option. I could walk away from the job, or they could press charges."

"What charges?"

Leonard looked into his mug. "Reckless en-something-ment."

"Endangerment."

"Something like that."

"You should have waited for a lawyer."

Leonard laughed. "You hear that, Stan? I should've waited for a lawyer."

Stan crossed his arms over his chest, grinning like a Buddha. "He would've waited a long time, miss," he said. "A real long time. He did the right thing."

"You don't know what it's like. In that room alone. No family. No friends. Just the police pushing you with questions. Just you and them in that little room. You don't know what it's like."

"Actually," Rachel said, finishing her tea, "I do. I've been there."

"Been where?"

"That little room. In the police station."

"Damn," Leonard said, rocking backward on his stool. "Aren't you full of surprises? And I thought you were a nice girl. What they want you for?"

"Same as you. Questions. Blame."

Leonard shook his head mournfully over his mug. "Babylon," he said.

"What?"

"That's what the Rastas say." He pantomimed taking a deep drag from an invisible joint and in a stage Jamaican accent said, "It's Babylon, mon. Babylon."

Stan glowered from his end of the counter. "Don't mock what you don't understand," he said.

"I ain't mocking," Leonard said. "And I understand it perfectly well. This?" He raised his arms, palms to the sky. "We're in exile here. This place of darkness. Not *this* particular place, of course," he said to Stan, "but in general, all over. Babylon." He turned again to Rachel. "You know what I don't get about cops? Okay, sure, they have a tough job. But what kind of a person drags in a sister who's just seen . . . I mean, that's cold. Body's not even in the ground."

"No," Rachel said. "This wasn't last year. Last week."

"Last week?"

"An officer came to my booth, asked me to come to the station."

"You should've waited for a lawyer," he said, smirking over the lip of his mug. He took a sip and made a face. "How is it that it's so good when it's hot but disgusting when it's cold?" He put his mug down. "The timing's strange. Why now?"

"I don't know," Rachel said, both hands on her tea. "I thought they wanted to ask me about the graffiti, but that's crazy." She told the *Don't fall* story to Leonard.

"It's the motto of the year," Leonard said, "don't fall. Remember the kid who fell off the jetty last winter?"

"Waters?" The name had stayed with Rachel—the boy who had carried his fate with him from the moment he was born.

"Yeah." Leonard signed the air, signaling Stan for the check. "There are rumors."

"Such as?"

"Maybe he didn't just fall. Maybe he jumped."

"Killed himself? Why?"

Leonard's head slumped into a gulf between his shoulders. "Broken heart, some say. Over a girl."

"Who?"

"Does it matter?"

Rachel liked to think so. From the radio, the deejay invited listeners to hold someone they loved and dance to the music, a waltz as soft and liquid as a lullaby. A ghost dance, Rachel thought, for the Make-Believe Ballroom. She imagined a mirrored ball turning slow laps of dappled light on the walls, glowing figures rotating in the dark, faces that would appear and disappear with the turns.

"This Waters," she said. "His father works in the parks?"

"Used to," said Leonard, fishing in his pocket for cash. "Stone gave him the boot after the coaster accident."

"A fall guy."

"One of them," Leonard seemed to lose himself in the bottom of his mug. "He had a brother too, this Waters kid. Younger. Name's Ethan, I think."

"They leave town?"

"The mother took off. But the father and son? They're still here. There's something about this town that sucks you in and holds you. A vortex. Hell, Ethan is still on the boardwalk. A fried food stand. You know which one? You ready for this? You ready?"

"Not the Sizzleator?"

"The Sizzleator. Can you believe it?"

"Do I have a choice?"

July 19, 2013

There's no alcohol in Sea Town, but that doesn't mean
people can't bring it with them. The liquor store across
the bay doesn't hurt for business. Tourists take the
booze to their rentals, and mostly it stays there. But
every once in a while, the drunks like to wander, and
when they do, it's to the beach or the boardwalk. Last
night, they came to the Moon Walk.

It was a bad mix—two guys, two girls, and a huge
plastic sippy cup I'm sure was filled with vodka and
bullshit. That's the way it always is—alcohol you can't
taste hiding inside a sugary drink as innocent as a
cherry freeze pop. You down it like soda and then—
bam—it sneaks up from behind and smacks you on the
back of your head.

At first, this crowd wasn't too bad, just loud. But
their language was crude, and they were making the
other customers anxious—parents rushed their little

Jennies and Johnnies through the course to put some distance between them and the rowdies.

So far, so good. Just something you note and set aside, because most of the time, nothing comes of it. Amy, who was serving her shift on a stool by the back holes, kept her head low: see no evil, speak no evil. I exchanged glances with Tango, who merely shrugged as if to say, shit happens—you can expect some of this now and again.

But then one of the guys, a bruiser in a red sleeveless shirt who commanded the giant cup and through it, his gang, started hooting something about a wet T-shirt contest to a cluster of girls by the fountain obstacle. His crowd laughed; the girls did not. They began to knot around each other in self-defense, and I could feel the climate change, a kind of steel chill in the air.

At this point, the fairy tale princess felt compelled to step in. I hung back by the office, watching out of the corner of my eye.

"Please," Diana said. "If you're disturbing the other customers, I'll have to ask you to leave."

"Who am I disturbing?" the bruiser said. "I'm just playing. We're having fun."

"Just keep it a little, you know," Diana said, pressing the air down in front of her with her palms. Let the genie go back to his lantern.

It should have ended there. But like I said—the sweetest drinks are the sneakiest. This guy was on the spot in front of his friends and couldn't let it go. "We'll keep it the way we want. We fucking paid to play here, and we're going to play just like all these other people," he said, swinging his arm in a loopy circle.

"You're welcome to," Diana said. "Just keep it down."

"And if we don't want to?" the guy asked.

One of his girls plucked at his shirt, saying they should go. She said the place sucked and they should just go.

Of course, her attention only made things worse. Muscle Head stood on principle: they paid for their tickets, just like everyone else. They had rights.

There were four of them and one of Diana. Amy deliberately looked away, pretending to keep watch over a pair of twins struggling with the crater hole near her corner. Tango met my gaze. He spoke before I even reached him. "This is a management issue," he said, putting up his hands. "Don't you think management should manage it?"

I had started to say something about all of us being in this together when I heard Diana fall on exactly the wrong words to say at the wrong time. "I don't want to make you leave," she said to Muscle Head.

At once, the mood of this little group shifted into something more sober, even grave, their eyes reflecting a sense of caution. I had a feeling they had been through this before—and they didn't care to see what would come next. Muscle Head pushed the shirt plucker from his side, asking Diana just who the fuck she thought she was. Diana responded so softly, I couldn't hear what she said. With her hair falling over her face, I could just barely see her. The quieter she was, the louder Muscle Head became, waving the club in his hand, challenging her to "go ahead, call the police, call!" while the other guy in his group, two deferential steps behind him, grinned into the ground, his hands in his pockets. The girls made a game of turning to leave but, aware that no one was paying attention, turned back again.

"You going to call? Call!"

Diana lifted a hand to push the hair from her eyes, and Muscle Head, startled, took a sudden step back. One of the girls giggled. His face reddened. For a moment, he was a bundle of twitches struggling to control, or surrender to, the competing impulses under his skin. One of them had to triumph, and when it did, Muscle Head took a poke at Diana with his club. Not hard. Not a swing. But a poke. Right between her breasts. It all happened so fast—his movement, the girls' shrieking, the sidekick behind him saying, "Whoa, hold up, hold up." But in all this, one thing hooked me: the expression on Diana's face. It wasn't fear or anger exactly—it was the look of the abandoned, of a person with a sudden grim awareness that whatever else was going to happen and whatever would come of it, she stood alone.

I'm not a brave guy by any measure, and all this time I'd kept hoping the whole thing would blow over, that one person or other in this party of idiots would have the sense—or the strength—to take this guy by the arms and lead him outside. I had watched and waited, silently hoping, until I saw that poke and caught Diana's eye, a look that was neither a call for help nor a call for blood, but just a call. Out of nowhere, I snatched the club from Muscle Head's hands, looked him in the eye, and told him it was time for them, all of them, to leave. Right now.

A vacuum of silence. I could feel my heart beating in my throat, and my face tensed into a knot, expecting a fist in it any second. But there must have been something in my voice that meant business because they left. They left noisily. They left with a parting shot, throwing their plastic cup, lid, straw, ice, and all, into the fountain. But they left. I followed them out, then without thinking about my pants or shoes or anything, stepped straight into the fountain to fish out the mess they had left behind.

When I climbed out, Diana was beside me, holding a towel—I have no idea where she found one—and when she handed it to me, our hands touched, and that triggered it. All the nervousness and fear came rushing to my eyes. I buried my face in the towel and turned away—a child's way of becoming invisible.

"That was scary," Diana said.

I pulled the towel from my face. "Yeah," I said.

"But we managed."

"I guess we did."

I thanked her for the towel, and she told me my sneakers were leaking. She was right—they were making little black puddles on the walkway—and I said they weren't leaking, they were crying because they had been so scared. And Diana laughed.

Lying in bed, I replayed the scene over and over in my mind, pausing, always, at her laughter, the kind of music it made.

what's left behind

Robert Leary of Wichita liked yard work because it gave him a sense of accomplishment. His wife, featured in all his photos, had a milk-fed plumpness and a ready smile.

In Portland, Oregon, Bobby Leary worked part-time in an auto parts store while getting his songs together for YouTube. He had some kind of Celtic tattoo on his upper right arm; under the picture, a visitor left a comment, "It's Irish for 'shithead.'"

In his comic strip, Sledge Leary found new life battling the ranks of the undead: werewolves, zombies, vampires. He carried a blowtorch now because the only way to keep the undead unalive was to cauterize their necks after tearing off their heads.

And Ethan Waters, Ethan Waters of Sea Town, New Jersey, had tons of pictures on his Facebook page. Pictures of him on the beach, pictures of him with his brother, Jason. And quite a few where his face was obscured by a pair of mirrored aviator glasses.

"I'm making new friends," Rachel said to Mrs. K, who held

her tongue, waiting for Rachel to say more. "One works at a go-cart place. The other at the Sizzleator."

"Either of them going to college in September?" Mrs. K asked.

The clock cat shuttled its eyes, left-right, left-right. Always and forever.

"Not likely," Rachel said.

"That's too bad."

"No, it's good. Why make friends with people who'll leave in another month or two?"

She left a note with the manager at the Sizzleator. She knew he was the manager because he wore a name tag that said so, gold on black. It was the one clean thing in the stand; too bad customers couldn't eat off it.

"Can I leave this for Ethan?" she asked.

"Sure." Given the eager way he had reached for it, Rachel was glad she had sealed her message in an envelope. The note began with two words: *Don't fall.* She told him where and when they should meet and that she would be the girl in the blue baseball cap. *I want to know why,* she wrote.

Rachel arrived early, positioning herself against the boardwalk rail where she could watch the front of the Aqua Arcade. It was unusually humid—the evening seemed set in a bowl of warm Jell-O. Streams of people crisscrossed in front of her, a parade of families and friends bumping shoulders as they walked side by side, their little collisions a kind of chorus of belonging. Rachel looked through them, waiting.

She wondered what Leonard was doing. And wondered why she wondered that.

At almost exactly nine thirty, a boy in an oversize concert T-shirt stopped at the front of the arcade, scanning the crowds.

Rachel shifted behind a cluster of excited teen girls; they had made their minor collisions too violent, spilling food and laughter over the boards, their bodies twisted in giggles and embarrassment. The crowd streamed around them. Ethan didn't seem to know what to do with his hands, which moved from his sides to his pockets and back several times as Rachel watched. Their eyes met. Startled, he turned to the arcade with his hands clasped behind him, seemingly engaged by a display of hermit crabs.

Rachel moved to his side, pretending to be absorbed in the same crabs that clung sadly to the chicken wire cage. A sign said the crabs were free—with the purchase of a complete "care kit." At the cage bottom, crabs scrambled over each other in impossible shells painted with cartoon characters, tie-dye patterns, sports team logos. Spider-Man had nearly reached the top of the cage when his claw lost grip and he toppled to the bottom again.

"Seems cruel," Rachel said, turning to the boy. "There's no escape, but you'd think they're entitled to a little dignity."

He turned to look at her, then pointed toward his brow. "Mets?"

"Yeah. Ethan?"

He nodded. "Why'd you cover the logo?"

"I'm not a fan," Rachel said. "Of the Mets or anyone else. I'm Rachel." She extended her hand.

He shook it tentatively, as if skeptical of its reality. Nearby, the Drop Tower ride hissed and roared; a half dozen riders screamed together, their legs kicking outward simultaneously, the limbs of a startled insect.

"You're not what I expected," he said. "I thought you'd be

taller, more . . . I don't know. I thought you'd be a Natasha or Marlene."

"Sorry to disappoint you."

"That's okay," he said, oblivious to her sarcasm. Then his mood shifted, dark and sudden, as if he had just found a smudge of dog mess on his favorite shoe. "What's this *Don't fall* mean?"

"I was hoping you'd tell me," Rachel said, watching him carefully. "I saw you. You and the pirate." She tried to make a joke of it. "Arrgh."

He didn't find it funny. "You tell anyone?"

"No."

"Are you going to?"

"No."

"Then what do you want?"

She wasn't sure. There was her curiosity about his graffiti—why did he do it, and what did it mean? Then there were the brothers. She and Ethan probably shared a common wish that theirs, at crucial moments, had kept still. If nothing else, he knew what it was to lose a brother and perhaps—if the graffiti was any indication—to resent the big silence in which he was buried. "You play Skee-Ball?" she asked.

The question seemed to catch Ethan off guard. He lifted his head. "Not in a long time," he said.

"Same here," said Rachel.

They found a row of open machines in the back of the arcade and chose two side by side. The air was dizzy with bells, spinning lights, the dead scent of burnt popcorn. Rachel made change at a machine that sucked in her five-dollar bill and spat out a clatter of quarters. She poured half of them into Ethan's hands.

Their coins released cascades of wooden balls that clacked neatly into their trays. Rachel rolled a few, thinking of what to say next. Without really trying—probably because she wasn't trying—she scored a hundred points with a casual roll that dropped into one of the two narrow cylinders in the upper corners. The ball shivered inside the tube as if fighting its way through.

"Good one," Ethan said. "That's the way I like to play it."

"I just got lucky," Rachel said.

In fact, after four or five balls, Ethan was ahead by thirty points. As soon as Rachel applied real effort, she racked up a series of gutter balls.

"It's all strategy," Ethan said. "I go for the hundreds in the corners. Even if you only get two or three out of nine, you're still doing good."

"You've given this some thought," Rachel said, rolling a ball that lilted too much to the left, bouncing off the edge of the thirty cylinder, sinking into the ten.

"My brother and I used to come here a lot," Ethan said.

"Jason?"

"Yeah. You knew him?"

"No," Rachel said. "I mean, I knew *of* him. I knew him by sight. But I didn't really know him."

"Me neither," Ethan said. "And I'm his brother. Crazy, right?"

"I'm sorry."

"Sorry for what?"

"Just sorry. I lost a brother too. On the Rock-It Roll-It coaster. Last year." Rachel picked up a ball and felt disgusted with herself for doing to Ethan exactly what she hated people doing to her: rushing in with words, filling in the blank spaces before the awkwardness grew, like vines, around them. She pretended to focus on the game. Her next ball arched gracefully into the fifty as if guided by radar.

"That's the way," Ethan said. They finished their set, Ethan ending sixty points ahead. "Nice job," he said graciously, though he couldn't disguise his pleasure with the greater number of yellow tickets that streamed from his machine.

Rachel challenged him to another round. They played intently, silently. Again, Ethan scored higher, but this time by only ten points. More tickets poured from their machines.

"What do you do with all your tickets?" Rachel asked, folding hers into her pants pocket.

Ethan said he put them in a box he kept under his bed. "I save them up."

"For what?"

"Depends. One year I wanted a laser-tag game. It was really cool. Came with two belts, two laser guns. But it cost twenty thousand tickets. Took me most of the summer to get to fifteen thousand."

"So what happened?"

A shadow, perhaps of regret, perhaps of some secret shame, crossed his face.

"I couldn't wait for the next season," he said. "Didn't have the patience, I guess. I got a clock radio instead. And you know what's funny?"

"What?"

"I didn't want a clock radio. I already had a clock radio. But it was exactly fifteen thousand points, so I took it."

Somewhere in the arcade, a teenage boy shouted, "You ditched it, man, you ditched it!" Another voice trailed behind it with a lot less enthusiasm. "Aw, shit," it said.

"What about Jason?" Rachel asked. Her next roll clanked the ball off the edge of the fifty, sending it sliding back down the ramp. She caught it before it dropped to the floor.

Ethan smiled. "He didn't get that many tickets. His strategy was all wrong."

"Why?"

"He rolled for the middle. He had this theory: play it safe and aim for the fifty," he said, pointing to the innermost targets. "And if you fall short, you stand a good chance of getting the forty or thirty. You keep steady, and you almost never get a gutter ball."

"Seems wise," Rachel said.

Ethan shook his head contemptuously. "He never got the big scores," he said. "I beat him almost every time. My brother would get so mad."

"Got ya," another voice said behind them. "Luck, sheer luck," someone else said. "Not luck, my friend," the first voice replied. "Mad skills, my mad skills."

Ethan held a ball with both hands, level with his chest, as if he were about to make an offering of it. "He mentioned it, you know."

"Who?" Rachel asked, confused. "Mentioned what?"

"Jason, the accident."

"The roller coaster?"

The arcade seemed to evaporate, as if everything around them had fallen back behind a secret wall for safety. "He said something to you?"

"No," Ethan said, rolling his ball up the ramp. "Not exactly. He wrote it down. In a journal."

"A journal?"

Ethan nodded his head. "I shouldn't be reading it, right?"

"No," Rachel said. "You should. It's what he left behind." Better, she thought, than a pillowcase full of seashells. "I'd like to read it. The part about the accident, I mean."

Ethan looked away, torn between silence and speaking. Rachel had seen this before with Curtis. Because of his bullheaded style of walking—head down, brows furrowed—Curtis had a way of finding things, like loose change, missing earrings, and puzzle pieces. For him, it meant the excitement of discovery. For Rachel, it meant vigilance, directing him away from lamppost collisions or outside the sweep of active swing sets. When he found something, his excitement was immediate and all-consuming; the world around him dropped away as he focused on the one thing that mattered, the thing in his hands. Although his enthusiasm was frankly exposed, getting him to reveal his find was something else entirely. Like a four-year-old, he would cup the coveted treasure with both hands and twist his torso aside to conceal his prize. Cajoling was useless; brute force was out of the question. But even if she could deny her own curiosity, Rachel couldn't ignore the danger. As often as not, the prize was a filthy piece of chewed gum or a ragged shard of broken glass. Over time, she had learned to forgo the frontal assault for a flanking maneuver: shift his attention to something else, get him moving, and then he'd voluntarily open his hands.

Once, Rachel's patience had been rewarded with something truly remarkable, a robin's egg as blue and inviting as an August sky after a sudden storm. Though he didn't know what it was, Curtis cradled the egg in his palm intuitively, the champion of its fragility. Rachel explained what it was, and Curtis's eyes grew wide in anticipation of the extraordinary bird that would eventually peck free from its shell. But when Rachel allowed Curtis to carefully tilt the egg into her own hands, she saw something he hadn't noticed: a hairline fracture that almost certainly meant this bird was lost. "You know," she had said, "the right thing here is to return this egg to its nest; its mother will be looking for it." Curtis looked almost frantic, imagining the sorrowful mother searching hopelessly for her lost child. He nodded assent. Rachel made a show of burrowing into a nearby hedge where, with a regret she could still taste, she scraped a shallow hole with the heel of her sneaker, buried the egg, and concealed the crime with fallen leaves. She remembered squinting when she broke free of the hedge into the stinging daylight. "It's home now," she had said.

"Listen," Rachel said, taking Ethan by the elbow. "Let's get a prize." She led him to a counter at the back wall. An attendant, rigid with boredom, sat cross-legged on a high stool. In front of her, a glass case held plastic trays of knickknacks—candies, whistles, plastic animals—tagged with numbers. Behind her, the wall was draped with bigger items labeled with bigger numbers: stuffed animals, computer games, electronic toys.

"You want that laser tag?" Rachel whispered, watching the attendant from the corner of her eye.

"I don't have enough points," Ethan said.

"Don't worry about the points."

Ethan looked at her suspiciously. "I'm too old for laser tag," he said.

"Something else, then."

"You're going to give me your tickets?" Ethan asked.

"Something like that."

He put his hand to his chin, stroking whiskers that weren't there. "An iPhone case," he said, pointing to one on the wall.

Rachel knocked his hand down. "Don't point," she said. "Just tell me. The red one on the left?"

"Yeah."

Rachel almost laughed. Curtis would have picked the same one—the deepest red, the loudest color. And it also happened to be in arm's reach. She pulled her tickets out and pressed them into Ethan's hands. She nodded her head toward the attendant. "Get her attention, pick out a bunch of small things. Over there." She pointed toward the far end of the glass case. "And keep her busy."

Ethan looked at the tickets in his hands. "There isn't enough for the case," he said.

"Doesn't have to be," Rachel said. "You're buying a distraction."

Outside and a few blocks south of the arcade, under a shelter designated for smokers, Rachel opened up her hands for Ethan, exposing a ruby-red case in a hard shell of clear plastic.

"Holy shit," Ethan said. "I can't believe you did that."

"This'll be our secret," Rachel said.

"Holy shit."

"The first of many."

July 25, 2013

At first, Diana thought I was nuts. But I figured if anyone caught us, so what? "It's your kingdom," I said.

"It's my father's," she said.

"Same difference."

She had the keys, she had the alarm codes—and I can find my way around the park blindfolded. Considering how dark it was, that was a good thing. It was weirder than I expected, Happy World after hours. Without people around, it felt deader than dead—the frozen rides seemed to sulk, a party of wallflowers waiting for someone, anyone, to start dancing.

"I'm getting kind of creeped out," Diana said, holding on to my arm. "And I don't think my dad would be thrilled."

"That makes it even better," I said. A father's disapproval—it's the Tabasco sauce of love. A sharp right after the Pharaoh's Fury and just past the Claw, I found our destination: the Magic Carpet. You lie facedown on a platform, the "carpet," suspended from an armature swinging out from a rotating column. Once in motion, the carpet rises and falls as the arms turn. I've long admired it as a machine, but to be honest, I hadn't ridden it before. I said as much to Diana, and she said the same was true for her. When she was little, sure, she went on the rides. But she hadn't been on them for years.

Because she took them for granted? I asked.

She said it was something like that. "Maybe it's more about familiarity. You know, breeding contempt."

But I talked her into it, painting a picture for her of how cool it would be in the dark, in the silence, when we had the park all to ourselves.

Then she asked about the dead man.

I was impressed. I had thought she kept the nuts and bolts of the park at arm's length, but she knew about the dead man. The way it's supposed to work, the rides just won't run unless the operator keeps a hand—or a foot—on the switch. If the operator takes a powder—or drops dead—the ride comes to a halt. That's the way it's supposed to be. But I know the work-arounds the tech crews use to test the rides.

"Don't worry about the dead. I got that covered," I said. Once I worked my mojo on the operating podium, twisting the safety key while pressing the power and "sequence launch" buttons, we had thirty seconds to climb on our magic carpet, pull the safety cage over our backs, and lock our belts. Of course, the time pressure just made it that much more exciting. When we settled in, I reached for her hand.

"What if it breaks down in the middle of the ride?" Diana asked.

"I guess we're screwed," I said. "They'll find our bones in the morning. Side by side." I frowned, mocking the despair of the poor soul who might discover such a tragedy. "Very romantic."

She laughed, and just then, the ride jolted to life. I had turned off the lights and the sound effects that might've attracted attention. So it was just us, suddenly moving in the dark, an invisible hand lifting us from above, giving us a gentle push forward. We rose over the park fence, where we nearly brushed the adjacent motel, catching our reflection in a window blue with television light, then circled past a popcorn stand, a bend of Rock-It Roll-It Coaster track, and bare asphalt paths without their usual crowds. With each revolution, we dropped into the wink of a Sea Town streetlight and kept moving, the speed slewing our carpet out a little to the side, but never pushing us beyond an easy glide, a relaxed slicing of air, the kind of flight you'd make if you could open your arms and rise to the sky. Though the safety bars were between me and Diana, there was just enough space for us to face each other and, with a little effort, kiss.

The ride dropped into its deceleration pattern, easing us to the ground. I unlocked the cage and helped Diana off the carpet.

"That was amazing," she said. "I get it now."

"Why people like rides?"

"Why people like love."

I would've said it was the ride, but I knew from experience that Diana had the power to make me feel dizzy. A good dizzy. But now I needed to say something smooth, appropriate, in control—and all I could think of was the truth. "It's like everything falling into place," I said, pressing myself against her, sliding my hands into her back pockets. "For the first time. Like all the pieces coming together."

Diana touched my face, fingertips to my cheeks, then broke away to walk out of the park. "Let's get out of here," she said over her shoulder, "before it all falls apart."

claws

"I never really wanted a car," Rachel said, watching the grasses on either side of the road sway low and gentle under the brush of advancing headlights. "I just figured it would be another thing to look after."

"There's some truth to that," said Leonard. It was night, and the darkness sucked at the car as they drove through the marshes. With the windows down, the air tumbled inside, moist and salty. "Sometimes I think it's more trouble than it's worth. But then, here we are."

"Sometimes it just feels good to move," Rachel said, holding her hand palm forward out the window, pushing back the air.

"After a day in the booth?" he asked.

"After anything. I think that's the appeal of rides. In the parks, I mean."

"What is?"

"Motion. Motion outside ourselves, not like when you walk or run, but motion you're inside of."

"The spinning, twisting, falling thing?"

"Yeah, exactly."

"Huh," Leonard said.

Rachel admired his profile, the way he pursed his lips to put on his serious face. That was Leonard in a nutshell, she thought, the alternating layers of put-on and sincerity that left room for doubt while appealing for trust. Part of her advised distance; another part, the one that had drawn her into Leonard's car on a clingy summer night, wanted to enjoy the ride.

"I always thought it was the danger," Leonard said. "The make-believe risk."

The mock screams, the riders' "I'm not going on THAT thing" even as they're racing toward it—Leonard was right, Rachel thought. Give us danger, but not really. "As long as it stays make-believe," she said.

"Hungry?" he asked.

"A little."

"There's some monkey bread on the back seat."

"You think ahead."

"That's what I do." He knew back roads Rachel did not recognize, and soon they were off the familiar terrain of shy bungalows and bait shacks and onto narrow, unlit streets she hadn't seen before, the kind she had suspected were "back there" somewhere with broken porches and small, abandoned sailboats, their masts tilted cockeyed to the stars. In another mile, they had left pavement and were on a dirt road cluttered with pits and bumps, the headlights bouncing like fireflies off the bowing marsh grasses on either side of them. They crossed a low and narrow wooden bridge stained with bait and fish guts, and coasted into a clearing at the edge of the lapping bay. Leonard's headlights exposed a small knot of black steel cages tangled on the ground.

"Traps," Leonard said, stopping the car. He cut the engine, and Rachel let her eyes adjust to the dark, watching distant lights from buoys and electric pylons come into focus. While Rachel had anticipated the moment they'd park, it still felt abrupt, like an invited guest knocking at the door before she had finished dressing.

"You've been here before?" she asked.

"I used to go crabbing here with my grandpa."

"Did you catch any?"

"Tons. We filled laundry baskets with them. They'd scramble over each other, trying to get out. We put them in the trunk, and if we kept the radio off, you could hear their claws clicking away." Leonard clawed the air with his fingers.

"Creepy."

"Funny," Leonard said. "My grandpa, he had a knack for knowing just where to drop the traps. He said it wasn't the bait, but where you put it. I suspect he was teaching me some larger lesson, but damned if I know what it is."

They watched the lights flicker on the water. Rachel could hear Leonard breathe, and she wondered if he could hear her too. This would have been a natural time for a smoke, but he didn't reach for his cigarettes and, in fact, hadn't smoked all evening. She wondered how far he had planned ahead, what he expected or maybe feared. She could have asked the same of herself, but instead she hid behind the monkey bread, taking a few bites, although she wasn't especially hungry. A buoy clanged in the distance. Leonard's seat rustled, Rachel stiffened, then she felt something touch her hand. She jerked it back, crabs and claws still very present in her mind.

"Sorry," Leonard said. The alarm on his face was pitiable.

"No," Rachel said, afraid she had hurt his feelings. She reached for his hand. "I was just startled, that's all."

He laced his fingers with hers and smiled. "Sticky."

"Your monkey bread."

"Guess I didn't think things through far enough."

"I'm guessing you did," Rachel said. She thought of the journal she had read, of the author who had always thought things through. Or almost always. "Let me ask you something. Suppose there were someone special in your life . . ."

"How do you know there isn't?" Leonard asked mock indignantly.

Rachel squeezed his hand. "Real or imagined. It doesn't matter. Suppose you had the keys to the park and could get in after hours. Would you take her on a ride, just the two of you?"

"It depends," Leonard said. He turned his head to the windshield, the black bay with tiny speckles of diamond light.

"Depends on what?"

"Lots of things. How likely I'd get caught, for example. The girl, of course."

"Let's just say there's no chance of getting caught, and the girl's willing."

"I don't know," Leonard said. "You have keys or something?"

"I'm talking hypothetically."

"Okay. I guess so, hypothetically." His head was bowed now, over their locked hands. Rachel couldn't see his face for all the hair that cascaded over his brow. "I'd just want to be sure there wouldn't be people around. Prying eyes and all."

"Suppose it's off-season—say, in the winter."

"In the cold? I don't like the cold."

"So much for romance," Rachel said, laughing. "Creature comfort comes first?"

"Comfort's got nothing to do with it," Leonard said defensively. "I'm as romantic as the next guy. More so. I wouldn't worry about me. I'd worry about the ride."

"Why?"

"The rides can be temperamental." He looked up, met her eyes. "In the heat, parts can swell or jam. We always have to be careful. There are always these little adjustments the maintenance guys have to make."

"Heat wouldn't be a problem in December," Rachel said.

"Cold makes its own problems. The cables get stiff. The chains get sticky. And then there's ice."

"So?"

"Ice can jam things up. It's unpredictable. And when you're running a ride, that's the last thing you want. No," he said, unlocking his hand from hers, lifting it up to her cheek, "you don't want the unpredictable."

"Well, we're safe, then. After all," Rachel said, leaning into Leonard for a kiss, "we're just talking hypothetically." His mouth was hot and tasted of mint and monkey bread. His hair swept over her face, shadowing her, and although it was night, she felt a morning mood, a rising-sun lightness of heart.

Several days and a few car rides later, they were in the Pirate's Playground booth, where "together" was against the rules. Rachel knew better, but Leonard had made a game of popping up from under the barred window, then tapping at the base of the air conditioner, then scratching at the door, and Rachel, unable to get rid of him and uneager to let him go, thought it safer to invite him inside than have him seen hanging around the park. She opened the door for Leonard's sly smile, welcoming him and their conspiracy of two. Once inside, he reached for her waist. She squeezed his hands, kissed him quickly on the mouth, then pushed him away, smiling.

"Stay out of sight," she said. "I can't have any trouble."

"I'm not making any promises," he said.

"Look." She passed him a memo, printed with the pirate bear arrgh-ing at the top of the page, that "wished to remind" park employees of park policies and park rules about friends and family: the privileges they had and, more important, those they did not. "Ours is a welcoming environment," the memo intoned, "but it is also a business." Employees could purchase discounted tickets from the office, but under no circumstances were they to admit anyone to the attractions for free. "Abuse of our policies," the memo concluded, "would be grounds for dismissal."

Leonard shrugged. "Same old, same old," he said.

"Look at the bottom of the page." Beneath Bobby Stone's name, there was another, Diana Stone.

"Preparing the succession," Leonard began. He would have said more, but Rachel had him duck under the counter as a customer approached the glass. She sold a packet of tickets, and Leonard took the liberty of tickling her leg. Rachel gave him a gentle kick. But with a left hand no one could see from the other side of the glass, she tangled her fingers in Leonard's luxuriant hair. The booth grew warm with silence. Another customer came as Leonard's hand crawled above her knee. She kicked a little harder—but not much. A line formed at the window, and just as Rachel greeted the closest customer with the least perturbed "can I help you?" she could manage, Leonard planted an electric kiss on her bare calf. Letting Leonard in, Rachel realized, was much easier than getting him out. When the crush subsided and the line cleared, she broke the spell and seized the opportunity, after another quick kiss, to push Leonard out the door. "Good riddance," she teased over his shoulder.

"Don't think," Leonard said, "that it'll always be this easy."

August 14, 2013

You know, you spend years thinking about it, dreaming about it, fantasizing about it. It's the hot mist behind your eyes, the big red door you can't wait to burst through. But sex isn't just an event with lots of moving parts. By definition, you have company. You have to go together and when you do, you might feel something you forgot to expect: a heartbeat other than your own.

I'd say it was Diana's idea if I hadn't been thinking about it since we started going together. But while it may have been on my mind, Diana's the one who made it happen. We were just goofing around after our shift at the Moon Walk, making out in the office before we locked up. "My parents are away," she said. "A friend's daughter's wedding in Cherry Hill. What do you think about that?"

She was doing that thing with my ear, making me crazy. I managed just enough clear thought to bring up the hour. Wouldn't they be back soon?

Nope. Staying at a hotel.

My hands were under her shirt, surveying the terrain, tourists loving the trip. "So you got the house all to yourself?"

"Not necessarily," she said, pulling out my hands. She seemed to be examining my nails. "Maybe I'll have company."

"Really?"

"Yeah, really."

I felt like an idiot saying it—I mean, this is something you should never have to say to a girl who wants to sleep with you: "I have to call my parents."

She gave me the look I deserved.

In my defense, I said they would be expecting me.

"Improvise."

I got out my cell and said I was crashing at Tango's. Given that this is my last summer before college, the 'rents have been cutting me some slack lately. My father cautioned me not to drink too much. "You have work in the morning."

"That's okay," I said. "I'm tight with the boss."

"I wouldn't count on it," he said.

We both walk to work—neither of our homes is far from the boardwalk. Hers is much closer to the ocean, right on the bulkhead facing the sea, an enormous pile of shingles, columns, and gaping windows. It wasn't a long walk, but it felt long, and thinking about what was

up ahead made walking difficult. I waddled like a duck—
an endless source of amusement for Diana.

Her house was dark, and we weren't inclined to turn
on the lights. Instead of going to her room, we hung
downstairs; with the lights out and the view out the
glass doors, it was as if the ocean had joined us in the
living room. Diana spread a comforter on the floor and
motioned me next to her. This is it, I kept thinking. This
is it. But I couldn't move. And with her hands under her
haunches, she seemed as awkward as I was. Afraid to
face each other, we both looked toward the ocean,
sitting as still as statues.

"This is silly," Diana finally said. "It's us,
remember? Us."

"I have no idea what I'm doing," I said. "You better
lower your expectations."

She lifted her shirt up over her head. She must have
removed her bra when she went upstairs for the
comforter. I've felt her breasts before, but I've never
seen so much of her skin all at once, never seen anything
more beautiful in my life. A word popped into my head
that seemed so out of place yet so right: "generous." She
was being generous, and I wanted to drown in her.

"Whatever happens," she said, "it'll be great."

But I couldn't lose sight of the details. I warned her
that I didn't have any condoms.

She reached behind her and held one up in the air.
While I was dizzy with love or lust, she had kept her
head and made calculations: blanket, bra, condom.

"You think of everything," I said.

"Now I'm tired of thinking," she said, leaning, practically falling into me, her arms wrapping around my back, her fingers twining into my hair. . . .

At first, it was awkward, fumbly. Then everything clicked, and she was right. It was us. It was always us. It remained us. And there was her heartbeat over and above everything else.

For a long time, we just lay there, playing with each others hands, saying nothing. "God, your father would kill us if he knew we were seeing each other," I said.

"He's not the murdering type," she said, "much. You, he'd just fire. Me . . ."

"What about you?"

"He'd be disappointed. Very disappointed."

The way she said it, it sounded like it had already happened, as if she were carrying a big sack of his disapproval over her shoulders.

"We should go for a swim," I said, changing the subject. It just popped into my head, not even as an idea, but more as an image, the two of us bobbing in the dark water, distant lights winking at us on the wave caps.

"I thought you hated the ocean."

"I do," I said. "Or I did. I just thought . . ."

"Yeah."

We didn't go anywhere.

timmies and tiffanies

Even from a hundred yards' distance, it's easy to see the signs of a tragic boardwalk spill. The food itself—the overturned boat of fries, the lost funnel cake—will not be visible, but it doesn't matter. The rise and fall of alerted gulls, their startled wings and hostile caws, point the way. And the rupture of the crowd, the collective parting that bends around the loss to avoid collateral damage from the gulls overhead, draws even more attention to the otherwise unseen disaster.

It was just like that with the Stones. At first, Rachel couldn't see them up ahead as she came off her shift and made her way north on the boardwalk. But she noticed a bump, a bend in the stream of boardwalk strollers, and as she drew closer, the gull-like squall of activity became apparent too. Outside a pizza place, young men and women in sauce-stained aprons rushed around to produce shakers of garlic powder and crushed red pepper, to remove paper napkins from a holder that a large man with a booming voice had loudly claimed to be overstuffed.

Rachel recognized the man as Bobby Stone. The young woman standing at his side, conspicuously not frantic, but lean and quiet with a clipboard clutched in both hands, she did not know. Diana, Rachel assumed. When Diana picked up a wad of receipts her father had flung to the ground, and when she placed a pen in the fat hand that had reached back and wiggled its fingers impatiently, Rachel felt an abrupt sense of familiarity: this was what caretaking must look like from the outside, what others had seen when Rachel was with Curtis. She hurried on.

At her shift the following day, Rachel had the uncomfortable feeling the Stones might make her booth their next target. She made sure everything was in order and looked up expectantly whenever anyone approached. They never came, but at a quiet point in the day when sales were slow, she looked up from the book in her lap and saw a guy she recognized. He wore a baseball cap backward and seemed both eager to speak and unwilling to start. Then Rachel remembered: Phillies Fan from the Happy World roller coaster.

"You were right," Rachel said. "I found Leonard at the go-cart place. Thank you."

The gratitude made him uncomfortable. "Listen," he said. "About Leonard. You might not want to be seen with him."

"What are you talking about?"

"Just saying," he said. "The Stones are getting . . ." The right words eluded him. Then they just blurted out, as if escaping without permission. "When the Stones get nervous, everyone gets nervous. It kind of radiates from them, you know?" He put his palms together, then pulled them apart slowly, an antibenediction. "Like a pebble in a pond. Rings."

"So you're giving me a warning," Rachel said. "From the goodness of your heart?"

"It's not just me. It's everybody."

"Everybody?"

"No one wants this shit on their heads."

By the time Rachel could think of the next question to ask, Phillies Fan had swung away, out of sight and beyond earshot. She wanted to know more about what people thought was about to fall from the sky; she was frustrated by the hole that hung in the air.

"You know," Leonard said, "I think you may have mistaken me for a man of action. And that would be a big mistake."

Rachel, Ethan, and Leonard were sitting around a marble-topped table at Rose's in Atlantic City, a few blocks from Leonard's mother's apartment, where it was unlikely they would be recognized by anyone from Sea Town. Rachel had heard of it before, a doily-and-plastic-flowers kind of place with a menu as antique as a cathedral radio: Salisbury steak, Cobb salad, rhubarb pie. They were the youngest customers by two generations. Around their booth, klatches of chatty women with parchment skin talked amiably, squired by a handful of taciturn men in oversize polo shirts. At least, Rachel thought, she could expect a delicate teacup and saucer served with a steel pitcher of hot water at its side: fussy, yet functional.

But when the waitress came around to take their order, all

hips and heavy makeup, she said, "I'm sorry, honey. We're out of tea." Rachel was dumbstruck. How was it possible for a luncheonette, especially an old-lady restaurant, to run out of tea? "It's been that way for a week," the waitress said with wonder, as if addressing the inexplicable, like UFOs or the image on the Shroud of Turin.

Leonard ordered coffee and a bear claw; Ethan a Coke and something he found exotic, the mysterious dessert called "bread pudding." Rachel wasn't hungry but didn't want to sit at the table with nothing in front of her.

"Fine," she said. "Coffee."

"Breaking new ground," Leonard said, pointing his fork at her cup.

Rachel took a sip and winced. It tasted like boiled dirt, even with two packets of sugar and three half-and-half creamers. She wondered why people craved it. But it was hot and sweet and earthy, inviting a second sip, then a third. It made her feel more adult, and that feeling put her even more at odds with the complex map Ethan had unfolded on the table. Hand-drawn with different colored markers, each color representing various features of Happy World that Rachel found hard to follow, it was the template for an elaborate plan that would lead them into Stone's office and to what Ethan called "incriminating files."

"We'll play to our strengths," Ethan explained, moving objects on the map that represented their progress through the park: Rachel was a spoon, Ethan, the salt shaker, and Leonard, to his amusement, was the pepper.

"No stereotyping here," he said.

Ethan ignored him, dictating a plan of action that would involve Rachel stealing keys and Ethan getting alarm codes from his father (in some yet-to-be-determined way—alcohol might have to play a role). Leonard would scale chain-link fences and jimmy recalcitrant doors. "It's all about coordination and timing," Ethan said.

"I foresee a lot of spilled pepper," said Leonard.

"You think this is a joke?"

"I think," Rachel said, pulling her representative spoon from the map, "that this might be a bit more than we can manage." On the table, there was a skinny ceramic vase with a small vinyl rose bowing from its lip. She placed this on the spot Ethan had marked for the incriminating files. "Our best bet is Diana. You know her, right?"

Ethan shook his head mournfully, but it wasn't clear which he regretted—their rejecting his plan or his not knowing Diana. "Never met her," he said.

"Really?" Leonard threw a dubious look Rachel's way.

"It was a secret," Ethan said. "I didn't know Jason had a girl-friend. I don't think my parents did either."

"No one saw them together?" Leonard asked.

"Maybe no one cared to look," said Rachel. "But I don't see any way around it. We need to find Diana."

Ethan buried himself in his dessert, and Rachel watched him eat. Tempted to wipe a spot of pudding from his chin, she realized they had made a custody agreement by accident, the way, Rachel suspected, all truly important deals are made. He had consented to leaving the journal with her, at least for a while, to give her time to ferret out clues that may have been obscure to Ethan but might be obvious to someone older. But Rachel had failed to tell him that there was no guarantee she would see any further than he could; he had neglected to say that with the journal in Rachel's hands, Ethan would have a hold on her.

"Diana?" Leonard said after an uncomfortable silence. "You understand we're talking about Stone's daughter, right? What does everyone call her? The fairy tale princess. Doesn't that tell you something?"

"Maybe we don't need her," Ethan said. "We have the journal."

"Ah," Leonard said, drawing his palms together under his chin in mock obeisance, "the journal."

Ethan seemed poised to respond, spoon raised in hand, when the waitress returned with her coffee pot held high. She surveyed them carefully. For the first time, Rachel noticed that people at other tables were looking at them as well. "We okay over here?" the waitress asked.

"More coffee," Leonard said. "Please."

"Ladies first. Miss?"

"Sure," Rachel said, clearing her hands from her cup. She watched the way the waitress poured the coffee without spilling a drop, envying her casual mastery of the pot, the table, the restaurant's customers. It was all under control and with a light hand too—an easy grace.

"It's evidence," Rachel said when the waitress was out of earshot.

"Something in writing," Leonard said, rolling his eyes. "That changes everything. What I don't get is, why doesn't Ethan here just hand it over to his folks? Let them figure it out."

At the sound of his name, Ethan lifted his head, saying

nothing. He turned to Rachel for help, a familiar look in his eyes, a kind of question mark—or maybe a hook.

"He doesn't want to," Rachel said. "His mother's in New York, and his father . . . his father is kind of out of it."

"Chuck Waters?" Leonard asked.

"He's waiting for Stone," Ethan said. "To call him back in."

Leonard rolled his eyes. "Could be quite a wait."

"But we don't need to," Ethan said, poking his bread pudding. "We got Jason's own words. And you're an eyewitness to the accident. Instead of keeping all this to ourselves, maybe we should talk."

"Talk to who?"

Ethan shrugged. "The police. The newspaper."

"Whoa," Leonard said. "Back up." He leaned forward, head low, a cautious conspirator. "No one wants to stir the Sea Town pot. Everyone we know either works for Stone or depends on him one way or another. The police? The local paper? This is America's number one family resort. I know it is, because when I walk down the street, it says so on every other lamppost and in every other store window. You think anyone wants to think differently? Or if they do, you think they want all the moms, dads, Timmies, and Tiffanies who climb out of their minivans and poop money from one end of the boardwalk to the other to think any different? I don't think so." He looked into his coffee cup. "And that journal? What kind of news is that?"

"What do you mean?" Ethan asked. "It's all there in writing, his writing."

"But what's there in writing?" Leonard said. "Most people believe he fell. Some say he jumped. Now more people will believe he killed himself, and people who kill themselves are crazy. If they see any evidence, it'll be of mental illness, *his* mental illness. And Sea Town can go about its regular business of being hap, hap, happy."

Rachel grabbed Leonard by the hand. "Enough," she said. Part of her was disappointed in Leonard; part of her suspected he was right. "At least we know this for certain: there's more to the story than everyone thinks."

"So what?" Leonard said. "They've already cut me from Happy World. From most of Sea Town too. Why should I care?"

"What about us?" Ethan asked, implicating Rachel with a confident nod her way.

Leonard added a new stream of sugar to his coffee. "Maybe you should drop this whole thing and mind your own business."

"It is our business," Ethan said. "It's our brothers."

Leonard shrugged. "I'm ready to let go and move on."

"Move on to what?" Rachel said, releasing Leonard's hand. "People talk about moving on all the time, and I have no idea what the fuck it means."

There was a sudden pause, like a parting of waters, in the murmur of table conversations, the clinking of metal utensils. Heads turned. Leonard sat up straight, hands raised for a stickup, pleading innocence to the prying eyes around them. Ethan, embarrassed, returned to his pudding. Rachel lowered her voice. "Move on? It's like we're all waiting in line for something we can't see ahead, but there's always someone at our backs telling us to keep moving." She sipped her coffee. "I'm getting used to this," she said, indicating her cup. "It's not bad. Still not good. But not awful."

"What do you suggest we do, then?" Leonard asked.

"Who saw Jason last?" Rachel said. "All roads lead to Diana."

"You think she'll talk?" asked Ethan.

Leonard released a long, low whistle. "It's one thing to look for trouble," he said, "but it's another to track it down."

August 19, 2013

By the time my father got home, I had already heard about the accident in the form of rumor, misshapen whispers that proved, as they often do, too close to the truth. Word spread in waves, reaching the Moon Walk via Walter, who was only too happy to carry bad news.

Diana let me go to check it out. I asked her if she wanted to go instead, assuming she'd want to be there with her father.

She said she'd get the story soon enough. That probably made her the only person in Sea Town not eager to know more.

I wasn't able to get into the park myself—there were cops everywhere and officials with phones to their ears. Despite their efforts, a crowd bulged at the gates, a tumor of heads craning over shoulders, strangers exchanging guesses about what was going on inside. The buzz quieted when the cops cleared a path for a stretcher that rolled past surrounded by grim EMTs, their backs bent over the rails. In a brief gap between them, I saw a bump of white sheet.

"Dead," someone said behind her hand. There was a sudden intake of air throughout the crowd, as if it had become one startled body drawing itself to its feet. The EMTs rushed the stretcher down the ramp and into a waiting ambulance with restless blinking lights. We watched it pull away. Here and there were sobs for the unknown victim, and then a question: "What happened? What happened?" rolled through the crowd like a beach ball passed over stadium seats.

"Kid fell from the roller coaster," a man said firmly, an admonishment in its matter-of-factness. "A fucking horror."

That evening, I lay in bed drifting in and out of thin sleep, tangled in my own white sheet. It was around two in the morning when I heard my father come in downstairs.

He had an I-don't-want-to-talk-about-it look on his face when he saw me standing in the kitchen, but he didn't shoo me out. He opened the fridge and pulled out a carton of orange-grapefruit juice, his favorite. He drew two glasses from the cabinets.

I declined—too much acid too late at night. "What happened?"

Dad stared straight ahead, distracted, watching the film clip in his head. "Kid fell out of the Rock-It Roll-It."

"Jesus. How?"

"Damned if I know," he said, but I didn't quite believe him, and I'm not sure he believed himself. There had been problems with the ride that had cost him and his crew some late nights working under arc lamps swarming with moths. I'd been told to keep my distance, and my input was far from welcome, but from what I could make of it, it had something to do with the sensors and the safety bars. It was an elusive thing, a gremlin that would vanish for weeks, then pop up without warning, just enough of a problem to be a pain in the ass, but not enough, at least to Stone's thinking, to justify closing the ride.

"It should've been shut down." I hadn't meant to say it out loud, but there it was.

"'Should've' won't help us now," Dad said, looking into his glass.

"You talk to Stone?" I wondered if Diana was having a similar conversation with her father right now. For some reason, I imagined them in the living room, looking through the plate glass doors toward the ocean, as if the sea would tell them what to do and why.

"Someone's got to take the fall, Jason, and it's not going to be Bobby Stone."

I asked him who attended the ride.

Dad shrugged and said it was some kid. "He won't be enough. This is too big."

We avoided each other's eyes. "You think he'll blame you?"

"Already has."

"Are you . . . ?"

"Not yet. There'll be an investigation. They'll go through the motions." He swirled the juice in his glass.

None of this made sense to me. His getting the blame. Then this hanging on for what, weeks? Months?

"But if you're the fall guy, why wouldn't he just fire you now?"

That was too blunt, and I thought he might get mad. But he just shook his head pitifully. "You don't understand Stone."

"You're saying he's basically a good guy?"

"No, I'm saying he needs to see himself as a good guy. We all do."

"See Stone as good?"

"See ourselves as good. You know what he wants, more than anything in the world?"

"Money?" I asked. "Power?"

"Nah," he said. I think he was disappointed in me. "Legacy."

I'll be honest. I don't know if it was the hour or the shock or what, but I was having trouble following him.

He sipped his juice and winced—too much acid, even for my dad. He said Stone has already made his money and has all the power he can manage. "Now it's about what he leaves behind. To his kid. For Diana. It's got to be big, and it's got to be"—he paused, searching for the right word—"intact."

"What if she doesn't want it?"

"Well," he said, dashing the rest of the juice into the sink, "wouldn't that be tragic?"

circling the tanks

It always struck Leonard how ratty and squalid the little aquarium was at the end of the Atlantic City island. But why, exactly? Where was the precise rattiness? Was it the missing shingles, like gaps in a street drunk's mouth? The brown patch of scrub and picnic tables by the bay's edge, about as appealing as a scab? The way no one cared to restore the aquarium sign, the paint chips curling like dead leaves from the exposed plywood?

No, he decided, climbing out of his car. He chucked his cigarette onto the gravel. It was the whole sorry idea of the thing, the grinning cynicism behind it. School trip after school trip, he and his classmates, squirming impatiently in the windowless room they called a "Learning Center," had heard the same story of "the gift," of how the casino owners gave back to the community by building this (see the earnest learning associate lift her arms, see her make a present of all this to you, you underprivileged little boy and your underprivileged little friends), this aquarium. This place of education and recreation. This humble nod to the great sea surrounding the island and the citizens who lived beside it.

On the wall, there was a large black-and-white photograph of two well-dressed white men shaking hands, smiling into the camera. Gold jewelry leaked from the wrist of one man; disgust escaped from the eyes of the other. In this room, they would shake hands forever.

Shit—even in his thoughts, he dragged it out into two syllables, as if he were entertaining a friend sharing space in his head: *shee-itt*.

Because that's what it was, this halfhearted mausoleum of tanks and half-living creatures. A "gift" from men who couldn't give a rat's ass and didn't care who knew it.

And the strangest thing was, he knew she would be here, inside. He knew, not just because of the rumors he had picked up at the park like scattered litter from the ground, not just because it was whispered and wondered and weirded over. He knew, because he'd recognized her silver BMW and had the temerity to park beside it, practically cheek to cheek. He stepped back from the cars, admiring their proximity and their polar oppositeness, the one a luxury item, the other a beloved wreck. He patted the hood of his car—good boy.

It took less time than he expected. He found her in a great oval room of tanks, a dark and high-ceilinged room that nonetheless felt like the cramped underside of some tidal pool rock. Glowing water circled the room. Bored fish made circuits inside their tank homes. Besides himself, there was only one other, and although she faced the tanks, he recognized the blade-lean silhouette, the cramped stoop of her shoulders, the long drift of her hair on the back of her neck.

He approached, and when she turned, she spoke first. "Leonard Washington?"

"Washington. Washington Washington. Yup." His hands dived into his pockets. For all his clever, intuitive, knew-just-what-he-was-doing know-how, he had no idea what to say. He had figured he'd wing it and the words would just come. But they just didn't.

"Yup," he said again.

Since when had he become a country boy? He feigned interest in a tank, pressing a hand of lean fingers against the glass.

When she brushed the hair away from her face, the gesture made her familiar to him again, like the bite of a forgotten candy flavor from childhood. She wasn't exactly pretty—she looked too much like her father to be pretty—but, he had to admit, there was *something* there, a baby-bird something a lot of guys would want to scoop up and run home with. He just wasn't one of them.

"I never would've guessed I'd see you here," she said. "I mean, I don't expect to see anyone I know here."

He felt vaguely offended and didn't like the feeling. He preferred to be clearly offended, thrown something he could openly swing back against. "I'm just curious," he said, "about what's under the surface. Of the water, I mean. You?"

"It's just a place to go."

"As far north as you can go on this island without drowning?"

"Something like that."

They walked, Leonard marveling that in five years of working on the boardwalk, they hadn't said so much as "boo" to each other, and now it seemed perfectly natural that they would be circling this dark room side by side. He held his hands clasped behind his back. He could practically smell her riffling through *why*s in her head.

"Truth is," he said, "I came here looking for you."

The response should have been "why?"—and he had girded himself for that with a half-formed answer he'd smooth into shape as he spoke. But she didn't ask why, she asked how—how did he know she'd be there?—and when she asked it, he looked at the toes of his boots, feeling unexpectedly sorry for her.

"Oh, you know," he said. "People talk."

"They do," Diana said.

"Especially when you're—"

"The fairy tale princess?"

"You've heard?" Leonard asked.

"People talk." She managed a thin smile. It didn't last long. "You want something," she said. "You might as well get it over with and ask."

Again, there was that pity thing. Leonard tried pushing it behind his back, a troublesome nephew. "The whole thing with the roller coaster," he said, trying to find her eyes. "It wasn't my fault, and you know it. I want everyone else to know it."

"What can I do?" she asked, looking away.

Not honest, Leonard thought, not even close. It was the first check, an elbow in the ribs, against feeling sorry for her.

"Word is that guy who drowned last winter, you knew him. Knew him well."

No smile, no expression. She seemed to retreat behind her eyes. A toddler hobbled through the doorway, his arms waving for balance, followed by a young woman in a half-crouched run. "You!" she said hungrily, as if he were an escaped chocolate that had managed to make a break from the dessert table. She gathered him up in her arms, and they left as quickly as they had entered, the echo of their laughter hanging in the air.

"What are you talking about?" Diana asked, brushing hair from her face.

"I'm talking about Jason Waters." He had planned to play miser with his cards, turning them only as he absolutely needed to, but now he spread them open and wide, like a tipsy tourist. "I'm talking Moon Walk, drinking on the beach, riding on the Magic Carpet."

Faint light from the fish tanks waved lazily over her face. "People tell stories," she said hopelessly.

"People do," Leonard said, playing his advantage. "But one person left a diary."

"Jason?"

Leonard nodded gravely.

"Have you seen it?"

Leonard's hands found their way into his pockets again. "Listen," he said. "I'm not out to get you. That's not Leonard Washington Washington's style. Not my way of doing things. But . . ."

"But what?" she asked, a hard knot in her voice.

"But I got to be free of all this shit. This Rock-It Roll-It Coaster shit. You know what I'm saying? Free of it."

They were in front of an especially dark tank. A formal label on the wall identified the occupant as an electric eel. A far less formal, more urgent message was taped to the tank. DO NOT DISTURB THE EEL, it said in handwritten capital letters—an angry protest from a would-be defender. Diana drew herself close to the glass, squinting into the murky water. "I don't know what you think I can do about it," she said.

Leonard stepped up beside her, looking in. "There are only two other people who know about this diary thing," he said. "But that can change." He shielded his brow with the cup of his hand and looked closer, scrutinizing the water for life. Finally he saw movement, a long supple s-curve. A satin banner of dorsal fin teased the water in waves that pulsed back and forth over the eel's spine. "It's supposed to be electric," Leonard said. "Does it ever light up?"

"Tap the glass," Diana said.

"What?"

"Come on," she said, meeting his eyes. "There's no one else here."

Leonard made a tentative fist, lifting it toward the tank. "I don't think we're supposed to do that."

"I won't tell. Go ahead. Tap it."

Leonard rapped his knuckles on the glass. With a speed that seemed impossible just a moment before when the eel appeared more to drift than to swim, an open mouth whipped toward the sound; a shock of light exposed a halo of hostile, pin-sharp teeth and two ruby eyes, like flares, blazing above them.

"Jesus," Leonard said, jumping back from the tank.

"Careful who you disturb," said Diana.

August 29, 2013

Tomorrow I'm going to Pittsburgh. This afternoon, I gave
Ethan a lot of the stuff I don't need, stuff my
grandparents gave me that I was supposed to learn from,
which I never actually used, stuff that would feel out of
place in a dorm room: a globe, three volumes of
condensed classics, a chrome desk set with pen, pencil,
and paperweight. Though the occasion might have called
for some kind of sentiment, it wasn't a warm and fuzzy
Hallmark moment. Ethan is too honest for that.

He asked me what he was going to do with "all this
crap."

I said something about gratitude and the lack
thereof, and he said, "Well, give me something to be
grateful for. Not junk you don't want."

He had a point. Right then and there I wanted to
give him something real, something good, but scanning
the room, I couldn't think of anything. He probably

thought I was being stingy when in fact I had just come
up empty.

"Nothing," I said. "I got nothing."

"That's all right," he said. "I get the room to myself.
That's enough."

Saying good-bye to Diana was harder. Much harder.
The more we talked about how we were going to see each
other again—and soon, and often—the less real it
seemed. We were on a boardwalk bench picking at a
couple of hot doughnuts gone cold, feeling frustrated.
Her parents, who were supposed to be out that evening in
Cape May, had made a sudden change of plans that
stole the house from us. I tried not to think about what
we were missing, but it wasn't working.

"Talk about bad timing," I said.

She didn't seem to hear me. "I envy you," she said.

"Why?"

"You get to leave."

"What are you talking about? You're leaving too."
She was headed to Fairleigh Dickinson, not because she
had any particular enthusiasm for staying in New
Jersey, but because it had a hospitality program.

"Not really. It's more like a pause. After four or five
years, I'll be back in Happy World."

"Is that so bad?"

"I know I should be grateful," she said. "And I am.
But."

I tried to be sympathetic. "It's a lot of work," I said.

"It's not just that. It's . . . it's lots of other things
too."

"Like what?"

A gaggle of seagulls poked around the crumbs at our feet. One of them looked up, anticipating a bite from the piece in Diana's hand. She saw the gull and began to conduct the bird's movements with waves of her wrist. "When my dad gets home from work, you know what he talks about?"

I shook my head. I had trouble picturing him as a man returning home, engaged in the casual business of pulling a snack from the fridge, picking up a remote, collapsing on a sofa.

"The injustice of it all," she said. Her entranced seagull chased a chunk of doughnut Diana flung away. "How he can never trust anyone. This one's lazy, that one's stealing behind his back. No one does what they're supposed to."

Including you? I wondered. But I didn't say. Just us being together was its own kind of answer.

"We have pictures," she said, gripping the bench on either side of her legs. "Black and white. What the boardwalk once looked like, before the Stones, way back when. The Pirate's Playground? That used to be a bowling alley. Where Happy World is, that was a ballroom and a couple of taffy stands. My great-grandfather started out roasting peanuts—Stone Nuts. Then my grandfather got bigger ideas."

"He built the first amusement park here," I said.

"And the second. And the first french fry stand. And the first mini golf." Diana smiled. "Before us, there wasn't much here but an ocean."

I laughed. "We owe it all to the Stones."

"You can thank my grandfather. Someone should."

"Your father doesn't?" I asked. I thought of my own father. After almost thirty years, he was about to be shown the door. "Your dad has a funny way of showing his appreciation."

"He doesn't appreciate, he resents," Diana said. She crumbled a bit of doughnut between her fingers. She said that back in the eighties, they almost went bust— grandpa had bought one stand too many, and the debt piled high. "My father never finished college. He came back and went to work."

"My dad too," I said. "About the same time." But he didn't have a boardwalk or a cute bear logo to show for it. He just had hope that everything would go back to normal, the sooner the better.

"My dad says the books were a mess, everything was a mess. Then a little bit at a time, one season after another, he built it up again. The way he tells the story, he did it all by himself." She lowered her voice. "I'm sorry," she said, "about your father."

"I thought they were friends," I said. "I just don't get it."

"What is it people say?" Diana asked. "That it's lonely at the top?"

"It can't be that simple."

"You think it's simple?"

For a long time, we didn't say much more. Diana threw the last of her doughnut in the air, setting the gulls into combat, and we got up to stretch our legs, walking aimlessly along the boardwalk. There was that strange, end-of-the-season vibe, as if magic carriages were about to turn into pumpkins. Stores that had gouged tourists all season were now marking down their crap by the day: 20 percent off, 25, 50. No one wants to be stuck with inventory that'll have to be stored all winter. And then find it's out of fashion next season.

The foreign workers, the "guest workers"—in their heads, they've already gone home. They're counting the hours and killing time exchanging text messages to friends and family in Israel, Russia, the Czech Republic. The people who own or manage the stands are all doing the math. How'd they do this season? Did they move enough shirts, boogie boards, hermit crab cages? Did they make a killing? Or just enough to coast until next summer?

We townies have mixed feelings. On the one hand, we all say we're glad to see the tourists go, to have the place to ourselves again, to have everything "back to normal." But the absence of crowds just means that summer's coming to an end and the days are growing shorter. And you know what "normal" really means, but no one will ever admit? It means three seasons of hoping that the crowds return next summer and that you'll be able to hang on until things pick up again.

That's the way it's always said: "when things pick up again." We all nod and understand without having to say anything more. It's our way. Our code. You get a coffee in the morning, shake the rain water from your jacket, and when someone asks you how things are going, you say you're holding on, you know, until things pick up again. There are three long seasons between summers.

"Don't you wish summer would never end?" I asked Diana, squeezing her hand.

"No. I wish it wouldn't begin," she said. "Summer's a promise that can't be kept." She looked out over the sea. "He suspects, you know."

"Who?"

"My dad. About you. And he's not happy."

"How'd he find out?"

"There are no secrets. This town's too small."

"What are you going to do?"

She kept her gaze out over the water, fixed and frozen. Paralyzed. I gave her hand another squeeze. It was time to say good-bye, at least for a while, anyway. Until Thanksgiving. Until Christmas. Until next summer.

"But there'll be phone calls and e-mail and texts," I said, trying to make the best of it. "It's not the real thing, of course, but it's better than nothing. Right?"

"Better than nothing."

"We got to hang on," I said. "Until . . ."

"Yeah," Diana said. "I know."

We were both crying. I walked her home. I looked at that big window facing the ocean, remembering how good it felt when we were on the other side, together, looking out.

"I'm going to miss you," I said.

She said she already did.

rachel's children

The best Stan could do was point Rachel to the right general neighborhood. "Leonard was a talker, that's for sure," Stan said as he wiped down the counter. "But he didn't have much to say about family."

Rachel wasn't sure which troubled her more: not finding Leonard or Stan talking about him in the past tense. It had been the same story at SeaSwift Go-Carts, except that the fat ticket clerk couldn't help but smile when he said he had no idea what happened to "old Leonard."

"He was scheduled for his shift, and he never showed up," the clerk said, absorbed once again in his Game Boy. "I haven't heard or seen from him since."

"That doesn't worry you?" Rachel asked.

"I got coverage," the clerk had said. "One goes, another comes in."

Stan, to his credit, was a lot less glib. "No, he hasn't been around," he said, reaching for a tea bag. "I thought, maybe, he was spending more time with his friends. Or at least one of them, anyway."

Rachel blushed. She pressed the tea bag into the bottom of her cup with the back of her spoon. "I haven't heard a word from him in days. It's not just me," she said quickly. "He hasn't been at SeaSwift, either."

"Really?"

"They say he just stopped showing up."

"Huh," Stanley said.

A party boat rumbled past the dock. On the PA, a man's voice corralled passengers for a line dance. "It's electric!" he said.

"The aunt, I think her name is Sally," said Stan. "Aunt Sally, that sounds right."

"Any idea where she might be?"

"Some. You know those apartments on the north end of the island, behind Memorial Park?"

"Vaguely," Rachel said. "There are a lot of them. Do you have a number?"

"Afraid I don't," Stan said. "But there'll be a ramp to the front door. A new one. I remember Leonard talking about it. He put it together himself."

"A ramp?"

"For a scooter." Stan straightened up from the counter, stretching out his arms. "This Aunt Sally is a big woman, you know what I mean? This electric scooter is how she gets around."

Rachel thanked him and reached into her pocket to pay for her tea.

Stan waved her money away. "Uh-uh," he said. "That's on the house. But if you find Leonard, you give him a shout for me.

Tell him Stan says to bring his sorry ass back here. And, hey," Stan said as Rachel was going out the door, "good luck."

Rachel feared a needle-in-the-haystack search among the dozens of buildings, each with four or six apartments, that made up the projects. But starting along the edge that backed the old evangelical campgrounds, she quickly spotted exactly what Stan had described: a low, black metal ramp that bridged a sandy patch of yard from sidewalk to doorway, two concrete steps up from the foundation.

The name on the mailbox was only modestly helpful: S. Collins. Beside it, a tan steel door was framed by two narrow, vertical window panes, each about the width of a hand and curtained inside with a kind of white gauze. Through them, Rachel could see the glow of an ancient television.

The doorbell croaked out a rattle that didn't seem to attract attention. Rachel knocked. A woman's voice from deep inside the apartment called out, "Who's there?"

"I'm looking for Leonard Washington," Rachel said through the door. "Are you Sally?"

There was no response, but through the windowpane, Rachel saw a scooter roll into the living room to face the door square on, as if prepared to charge like a knight on horseback. Driving the scooter, hands resolutely gripping the handles, was a large woman with a wide, pierogi face and blond hair combed straight back from her forehead.

"Leonard isn't here," she said hoarsely. "I don't want you people coming around anymore." The words sounded practiced, even tired, as if she had trotted them out many times before.

"My name is Rachel. I'm a friend."

"Leonard doesn't have any friends. Not in this town."

"Yes, he does. I know him," Rachel said. "His mother lives in Atlantic City. His name is Washington Washington."

On the television screen, a frieze of heavy traffic crawled between Philadelphia and the Jersey shore. A reporter's voice, surrounded by the whir of helicopter blades, said that now was not the time to leave for the beach.

"Lots of people know his name," the woman said. "We just want to be left alone."

"Please," Rachel said. "I'm Curtis's sister. The boy who died on the roller coaster."

The scooter seemed to rock back and forth, as if the driver was torn between advance and retreat. "They've already taken Leonard away," she said. "There's nothing I can do for you."

Rachel couldn't think of anything else to say. "Plan on leaving later tonight or first thing tomorrow," a desk anchor said. Then Rachel noticed something over his head, above the screen. "I gave Leonard the elf," she said. "On top of the television."

The scooter rolled forward and out of sight. For a moment, Rachel feared she had simply left the room, bored or exasperated by the presence at her front steps. Then the door cracked open. "You'll have to take this the rest of the way," the woman said, leaning over her handlebars. She gasped as she rolled back into her seat. "It's practically idolatrous the way he worships that elf."

They sat in the kitchen, where Sally had pulled a spread of luncheon meets and pickles from the refrigerator to the table. "If you ever told me I'd greet a visitor to my home so rudely," Sally said, placing plastic deli packs in front of Rachel and shaking her head. "But that's what things have come to." A sack of bread gaped open on the table. Although Rachel wasn't particularly hungry, she wanted to please Sally; she made herself a sandwich and offered to do the same for her host.

"Oh, no, thank you," she said, folding her hands over her belly. "Doctor's orders. I live on a rabbit's diet of lettuce and celery. Though you'd never know it by looking at me." She slapped her thigh, which jiggled under her sweatpants. "Leonard's got his mother's constitution. She's a beauty, you know. She looks just like me—except there's a whole lot less of her." She laughed.

"Where is he?" Rachel said.

"In God's hands," Sally said, sinking in her seat. "The county courthouse. In jail."

"Oh my God," Rachel said. Whatever appetite she'd had left. She placed the remainder of her sandwich on a paper napkin. "Why?"

"Why? I don't know. Lord knows I don't know." She turned her head to the stove, as if minding something cooking there. "It has to do with the accident. With your brother. Come here a moment, just shift your chair over."

Rachel slid next to Sally, who put her hand on her arm. It was warm and, though it was a large hand, light. "We're so sorry, you know. That's a damned terrible thing."

"It's okay," Rachel said.

"It's not okay. Not at all," Sally said. "Not by any measure. It breaks my heart. It does."

"But what's it have to do with Leonard being in jail?"

Sally rocked back on her scooter, which squeaked with the shift in weight. "Somebody's got to take the fall, you understand. There's got to be somebody to point to, somebody to take the blame so everybody else can go about their business. This time, Leonard's the one," she said. "They say he was negligent. Didn't follow instructions."

"They can't put someone in jail for that. What about a lawyer?"

"See that stack of papers over there?" Sally pointed to a pile on the living room couch—the same couch that must have doubled as Leonard's bed. "I've been calling social services this and legal counsel that," Sally said. "Let me tell you. No one's eager to take on a case that involves a black boy and drugs."

"Drugs?"

Sally nodded. "They did a blood test when they asked him questions. You know, after the accident."

"So what?" Rachel said. "I mean, Stone may have a lot of sway with the police, but even so, there's a limit. I mean, they're not going to forge the test results, right?"

"Oh, honey," Sally said, touching Rachel's arm again. "That's the thing. They don't have to."

It took a moment for Rachel to absorb what Sally had said. At first, she thought, why not? Would Stone forge them for himself? Then she understood. "He was high?"

"He was," Sally said. "And they're going to judge him hard for it. Hard."

"How could he be so stupid?" She hadn't meant to say it aloud.

"For someone so smart, it comes easily to him. It's a damned shame." Sally leaned forward. "Have some more of your sandwich."

"I'm not hungry, thank you."

"It doesn't do to be angry on an empty stomach," Sally said.

"I'm not angry," said Rachel. "I don't know what I am. Disappointed, I guess."

Sally's eyes were closed. She folded her hands and rocked her head. Her lips moved silently. A minute passed in a silence Rachel didn't appreciate. She was about to get up when Sally opened her eyes and said, "Try not to judge him too harshly. There's plenty of other people for that."

"And what do you think I'm for?"

"That's up to you," Sally said. "But you should know what's going on. They're threatening to throw the book at him. Maybe only some of it would stick. Maybe none of it. Just the trying will mean hell for him. But there may be a way out."

"What's that?"

"A statement, a signed statement. He has to say he failed to push the bars all the way down."

"And?"

"And that he saw your brother try to stand up. That's the deal. He says that, he signs that, and they promise to let him walk."

"What's he going to do?"

"Well," Sally said, backing her scooter out and around from the table and into the living room, "if he follows my advice, he'll do the right thing." She faced the television. "He'll sign the damned statement and come home."

Rachel returned the meats to the refrigerator and sealed the bag of bread. Fearing it would be an insult to leave the sandwich behind, she wrapped it in a napkin and slipped it into the pocket of her windbreaker.

As Rachel reached for the front door, Sally apologized for

the limitations of her hospitality. She asked Rachel to pray. "For Curtis and Leonard," she said. "Weep for your children, Rachel."

"What?"

"The Bible," Sally said. "Jeremiah 31:15. 'Rachel is weeping for her children. She refuses to be comforted for her children, because they are no more.' Do you find comfort in the Bible?"

"I don't find comfort in anything," Rachel said as she stepped outside, closing the door behind her.

On the foot of the ramp, she heard Sally's final word on the subject. "That's Rachel's destiny, honey."

December 13, 2013

It's Christmas break, and I should be feeling great, yet I feel anything but. If you had said three months ago that this was where we'd be, I would have said that was impossible. No way. Sure, we knew it would be difficult, our going to different schools so far apart.

"Only one couple in a thousand," people said. I thought for sure we'd be that one couple. Instead, we're part of the nine hundred ninety-nine. She hasn't said as much, outright, but that's where it's going.

At first, we talked a few times every day, then at least once a day. Then several times a week. But something just crept up on us and suddenly, we're only talking a couple of times a week—and she's hard to reach. E-mails go unanswered for days. Voice messages, unreturned. I thought, okay, we're both busy. But we're us. We'll always be us. Sometimes when we talked, the magic would still be there. We'd laugh easily, and then it would seem silly to worry at all. But those times have been getting farther and farther apart. Now, even when I reach her, she seems distant, distracted. I ask her if something's wrong, and nothing's ever wrong, but . . .

"I feel like I'm being torn apart," she says.

"By the distance?"

"By expectations."

"I just want you to be happy," I said.

She laughed, bitterly. "You sound just like my father."

Thanksgiving was a disaster. Family obligations kept us apart for the holiday itself. And she had to leave on Saturday. Friday night we went to a movie, got a cup of coffee afterward. We hardly had two words to say. I just felt heavy and lousy and angry, and I guess it showed.

"What's wrong with you?" she asked.

"What's wrong with us?" I said.

"You think there's something wrong with us?"

"Isn't there?"

A long, long silence. Even the other tables were quiet. I think people know when a couple's going south, because they gave us more privacy than we wanted. When we needed to be alone, we could hardly find a square foot to ourselves. Now people sit away from us. We're like an accident they don't want to see.

After we finished the dregs of our coffee, Diana said she had to get up early to go back to school. I drove her home. Our timing was awkward. When we pulled up to the curb, her father was outside stringing the neighborhood's first Christmas lights; her mother was steadying the base of his ladder, telling him it was getting dark already and they should get inside, for Christ's sake. I reached over to kiss Diana, and she gave me her cheek. Her cheek. "What's the deal?" I asked.

"Don't be an idiot," she said. "My parents. My father."

Last summer when we were a couple practically right under his nose, it didn't matter—we risked our secret recklessly, virtually ignoring him. Now that we're two campuses away from each other, he feels ever present, a hulking bear breathing outside our little tent. Diana was already out of the car before I could think of anything to say; I let the car speak for me, spitting a little tantrum of gravel from under my wheels. It made her parents' heads turn my way, but it didn't make me feel any better.

Right now, I'm sitting behind the oil tank in my basement. It was my haunt before I met Diana, and it's my haunt now. I don't want to see anyone, especially my family. "What's wrong with you?" my mother says when she sees me moping around.

"It's complicated," I said.

"At your age, nothing's really complicated," she said. "You just think it is. You want complicated? Just wait until you get older."

Great. It gets worse.

In about half an hour I'm going to see Diana, and in my heart, I know it'll be for the last time. She made the call, saying she wanted to see me. "We need to talk," she said.

"About what?" I asked stupidly. I already knew. "We need to talk" means "I'm letting you go." I got one concession: we're meeting at the park. One last ride on the Magic Carpet for old time's sake. I know it's corny, but if all I have left of Diana is a memory, I want that last memory of us together to be something worth holding on to.

Weeks ago I bought Diana a heart-shaped locket on a silver chain. I kept it simple: inside, it says "JW+DS." I wanted to add "forever" but there wasn't enough room, and as it turns out, that's just as well. I hadn't wrapped her gift until this morning because I liked pulling it out of its velvet box, squeezing open the heart, running the silver chain, like satin thread, over my fingers. Sealing the last fold of wrapping paper with a strip of tape, I felt like I was dying inside. Being with her was electric, a charge that made everything dance. Even the little things—a short walk, a shared box of caramel corn, a late-hour phone call just to say good night—all became fuller with her, like lungs drawing breath.

That's over. It's broken, and all that's left are the pieces. Nothing moves together in something bigger than the parts.

Now it's all just parts.

time to come back

At closing time, Walter stopped Ethan at the back door. "One more thing," he said.

"What?" Ethan asked. He looked around the Sizzleator. He had passed a mop across the floor and bleached the counters. On every flat surface, there was an oily sheen of grease that, regardless of what they did, never went away. But the place was as clean as it was going to get.

Walter reached under his apron and produced a lump of bills, all crumpled and squished, as if they had been forced into a hole from which they had failed to crawl out. He pulled a wrinkled twenty from the knot. "Here," he said.

"What's this?"

"Your share."

Earlier that day, Garrett and Mitchell had come by and refused to leave without a free basket of fries. They insisted he "share the wealth," and after some awkward near-arguing that threatened to disturb customers, Ethan gave in just to get rid of them. It was a small basket, a little boat, really, but it made him feel dirty: in the vast machinery of the boardwalk, he had become one of the greasy cogs.

"Nah," Ethan said to Walter. "I'm good."

"Not yet," Walter said. "I'm getting mine, and you should get yours. It's only fair." He shook the bill; it rattled from his hand like a snake.

"Really, I'm okay." Ethan tried for the door. But Walter beat him to it with a quick sidestep that blocked the way out.

"I'm not asking you," Walter said. "I'm telling you. Take it."

Careful not to touch Walter's hand, Ethan took the twenty, shoving it to the far bottom of his pants pocket.

"There. Wasn't that easy?" Walter asked as he opened the door. The night air swirled with little gray gnats. "Someday, you'll wish everything could be that simple."

That night, Ethan fell asleep with some difficulty. His one summer sheet came free from the foot of his bed and got tangled in his legs. He wrestled free from it and waited impatiently for dreams. They came but didn't last: at some point in the middle of a reckless run, he felt a hand on his shoulder that seemed to be shaking him out of his night world. The field Ethan had been scrambling in—leaping streams, dodging holes, climbing fences— dissolved instantly from open amber spaces into a dark shadow, like a fresh grave. He opened his eyes.

"Hey," his father said. "You awake?"

Ethan blinked at his clock. 1:54. "It's almost two in the morning," he said. "What's up?"

"I can't sleep," Chuck Waters said. "Move over." Ethan scooted to the wall side of his bed, freeing a space for his father.

"I've been thinking," Chuck said.

"Yeah?" At this hour, the prospect seemed dangerous.

"Things can come back together again. They will. I know things have been messy since—"

"I know."

"Yeah. All askew." Chuck made a tentative square with his hands, a ragged thing. He broke them apart again. "We've taken our hits."

"Mom?"

"Her too. Big time. It hurts," Chuck said, placing a palm on Ethan's brow. "It hurts that I haven't been able to hold things together. Keep us together."

"Not your fault," Ethan said, wondering where all this was going, fearing he wasn't fully able to follow.

"No, I deserve my fair shame of the blame," Chuck said. "I do. Maybe we all do."

"Maybe," Ethan said uncertainly.

Chuck removed his palm, clapping his hands together. "Got a call from Bobby Stone today, Ethan. A very interesting call."

Ethan kept still, holding his breath back on a leash.

"Very interesting call. You know, until a couple of days ago, he didn't even know you were working at the Sizzleator."

"Funny." But it didn't feel funny. Ethan found the sheet balled at the foot of his bed and drew it closer.

"Yeah, funny thing. He was looking over the books, you know, opening a few spreadsheets, and he saw something strange. Compared to last year, revenues at the Sizzleator have been down. But . . ."

"But what?"

"But Walter's been ordering the same amount of inventory,

even a little more. What could account for the difference? That's when he looked at wages and employees."

"Huh," Ethan said, glad that it was dark and that his father would have difficulty reading his face. "Is Walter in trouble?"

"Don't know," Chuck said. "Because that's not why Stone called."

In the fields he had just left, there were holes to climb in, rocks to hide behind. Ethan wished he were there now. He closed his eyes to see if he could find them again. Everything was blurry.

"Ethan," his father said, bringing his face down to him, brow to brow, his breath warm and sour. "Ethan, I have good news."

"What?"

"My old job. Stone thinks it may be time, time to bring me back."

"Really?" Ethan sat up with relief. "Really?"

"This could be the turning point, Ethan," Chuck said, sitting up straight, his face toward the bedroom door. "A new beginning. Your mom—"

"You tell her yet?"

"Not yet. Not yet. There's just one thing."

Ethan waited for it.

"Bobby Stone, he mentioned something about a journal. . . ."

chapter fifteen

rats

"Dan's asked me to move in with him," Betty said, just like that, without preamble or fuss. She and Rachel were sitting on the couch, watching a summer reality program neither really cared for; the dancers, the gowns, the applauding audience—placeholders for their attention.

"Interesting," Rachel said.

"I won't do it, of course," Betty said.

"We're a team."

"Of course."

"That was fast," Rachel said, thinking of the escalation of the romance. It was one thing to take a man to bed; it was another to have him take you into his home.

"Sometimes, when you know, you know," Betty said.

"Really? You love him?"

"I think so."

"Does he love you?"

"I think so. I don't think he'd ask me if he didn't. He has a nice place. Cozy. Has a deck facing the water. He built it himself."

"Handy," Rachel said. "Is there an extra room?"

Betty reached for the remote and turned up the volume. "You're so funny," she said.

Mrs. K said that people had a surprising capacity for renewal, for turning their lives around—she had seen it many times.

Rachel, who had never seen such a thing, shrugged it off as a consequence of age—if you lived long enough, you might see any number of extraordinary things, like double rainbows or rivers that had reversed their flow.

"No," Mrs. K said, "it has nothing to do with time. You see what you're able to see."

Or want to see, Rachel thought.

In Tucson, Bob Leary testified to being born again through the saving power of Jesus Christ. He grinned from the center of a family lineup, his arms outspread, not on a cross, but across the shoulders of a wife on one side and a daughter on the other. Two smaller boys were posted in front of them. They were all outdoors with a haze of desert mountainside at their backs, squinting into the sun as if there was only so much grace they could take.

The Robert Leary of Ottawa had become a motivational speaker, his bio said, to share the "unlimited strength" he'd found once he shed the interior deadweight that had been dragging him down. He had a ten-step process for Self-Renewal that began with Radical Honesty and ended with Welcoming Wealth. He generously invited site visitors to purchase a cornucopia of books and DVDs that would guide them on the path, all major credit cards (and PayPal) accepted.

Meanwhile, Sledge Leary was thinking of trading a lifetime of smashing things for a quiet cabin on a distant lake: what was the point of fighting the zombie hordes when zombie hordes were pretty much all that was left in the world?

"I wish you would put in as much time searching for *schools*," Mrs. K said.

"Sure," Rachel said. She reached into the cargo pocket of her pants. "I've brought you something." Biting her lip in anticipation, she watched as Mrs. K unraveled a skein of off-white tissue paper, releasing a candy-colored figurine into her palm: a little boy and girl holding hands, their cheeks pinchy pink and eyes ice-pick blue.

Mrs. K let it lie in her hand. She looked pained, as if the sweetness of the thing had given her a toothache.

"Well?" Rachel said. All day, in the booth, she had rehearsed in her mind the way she would say "you're welcome," how it was just a small way for her to give back, to return the favor, to show appreciation for all of Mrs. K's thoughtfulness over the years. She'd felt light-headed with goodness.

"It's lovely," Mrs. K said. "But."

"But what?"

"I can't take this." She returned the figurine to Rachel. "I know how you got it."

The figurine seemed to burn in her hand. "I don't know what you're talking about," she said weakly. Rachel was never impressed with her own skills as a liar.

"Curtis told me," said Mrs. K. "Sitting where you are now. He was confused. Me too. I thought about saying something to you, but I had hoped it was just a phase, something you would outgrow. So I didn't say anything. Should I have?"

You didn't want me to stop coming here with Curtis, Rachel thought. She put the figurine back into her pocket. Not knowing what else to do, she left, ignoring Mrs. K's pleas that she stay.

That night, Rachel lay awake in the dark, listening to small, scuffling sounds in the alley—the rattle of cans, the tinkling of jostled glass. For years, Betty had said it was raccoons, specifically, a family of raccoons. Thinking of them as a family of something made the noise less threatening, even endearing. But she had come to believe they were rats, not raccoons, and that even if they traveled in packs, their efforts were solo, each rat to himself.

Was it always that way? In the afternoon, a young couple had approached her booth with linked arms, hands slipped inside each other's ass pockets. They laughed and touched brows together. At the window, he asked for fifty tickets. When told it would be thirty-five dollars, he pulled a knot of tangled bills from his front pocket and found he did not have enough. She dug in as well, and the two of them made a game of compiling their cash, straightening out the crumpled bills, stacking them together. "Here," he had said, sliding the stack under the window. "It's all we got. I think we just made it."

Out in the alley, there was a mad dash of little feet—the flight of startled animals from a sudden noise, an unexpected burst of light. Then quiet again, an oppressive silence.

In the end, Rachel thought, it would be as it was in the beginning: she in a room, listening to her own thoughts, Betty finding a new home to grow restless in, Mrs. K content to grow old where she was. *As it was before, is now, and ever shall be.*

The figurine burning in Rachel's hand. And school, school, school—Mrs. K was obsessed with it. *But,* Rachel thought, *you can learn the things you really need to know just about anywhere.* For example, what had she learned in Sea Town this summer?

Lesson one: If a thing is worth giving, it's worth paying for.

Lesson two: Your esteem for a person is measured by how much you're willing to pay.

Lesson three . . .

Rachel fell asleep trying to think of one and dreamed about Leonard instead. He was imprisoned in her Pirate's Playground booth. He wanted to know why he was in there when she held the key that would let him out.

what you do with a broken shell

Ethan had a theory favoring plain sight as the safest place for hiding; if Rachel would meet him at St. Augustine's, she could return the journal to him there. By then, Rachel could have photocopied the pages she wanted, the pages referencing safety, park rides, and questions about the Rock-It Roll-It Coaster. Pages about the accident.

Sitting beside Ethan, groggy from the faint scent of old oak and incense and the drone of God's Word read in a voice as flat as the ocean's horizon, Rachel made another promise as well: no more games with Ethan or anyone else. Her frustration was tempered by the backpack between them—once she returned the journal, maybe she could let everything else go too.

"Well?" Ethan whispered. "Let's go."

"Can't," Rachel said between her teeth, fixing her gaze at the painting beyond the empty choir benches in front of them. "Too many people." If only Ethan had sat at the back, she thought. But no, the master spy had arrived early and sat up front where the morning mass crowd wouldn't pass him as they shuffled to their regular places among the middle pews. He hadn't considered that once mass began, they wouldn't be able to make a discreet departure until the services were over.

"Hoisted by your own petard," Rachel said under her breath.

"What?"

"Just keep still."

They rose from their seats for the gospel, then sat for the homily, the brief rumble of parishioners returning to their seats a kind of passive protest against the tired discourse that, Rachel was certain, would inevitably come. At Curtis's funeral, the last time she had attended a St. Augustine's mass, the priest had rambled through a homily that made a tenuous connection between the "mystery" of Curtis's life and the mystery of the Trinity illustrated in the church's choir painting, a work of art the priest never tired of referencing.

"Saint Augustine was a clever man, a clever man," the priest had said for what seemed the hundredth time, his bald head tilted over the papers he held, trembling, in both hands. Rachel had heard the story since she could remember and could virtually lip-synch it as it emerged, one familiar step after the other, retold with the enthusiasm of a man certain he was blazing a fresh trail: the clever Augustine writing about the Trinity; the frustrated Augustine walking along the beach, seeking inspiration; the distracted Augustine coming across a boy pouring seawater into a hole in the sand (here, the priest pointing to the painting, inviting worshippers to bear witness themselves); the witty Augustine telling the boy that he wouldn't be able to get all of the ocean into that little hole; and the surprised Augustine chastened by the boy's response, spoken just before he evaporated in a sudden mist,

"Just so, you'll never get all of the Trinity into that little book of yours." The delighted priest had chuckled softly to himself while the confused mourners looked to one another, seeking the invisible connection between Augustine's "clever" shock and their own stupefying grief.

The sun streamed through the stained-glass windows, illuminating the pews in garish circus colors. Rachel wiggled her fingers through the palette, tallying up the summer so far: Mrs. K disappointed, Betty in love, Leonard awaiting trial, Ethan recovering a family, and herself? If she stepped from the fog that had shrouded her these last few weeks, she would see that she had been distracted. It was natural, given the circumstances. But she had only herself to blame for not looking ahead. Other kids her age were packing up, getting ready for college. Maybe it was time to leave the past behind, to plan next steps. To move on.

So what was in her way?

An inability to accept things as they were. Accidents happened. Impulsive boys died. Foolish, brokenhearted teenagers slipped and fell. And the people they left behind tried to assemble wholes from pieces that were never meant to fit together.

They kneeled for the consecration. "He looks like you," Rachel said, lifting her chin toward the painting.

"The saint?" Ethan asked.

"The boy," said Rachel. "The blond hair. The puppy dog eyes. That air of determination. That's you all over."

Leaning forward, Ethan crossed his elbows over the back of the pew in front of him, resting his head in his arms, saying nothing. If people looked over, Rachel thought, they'd assume that he was praying.

They rose again for the Our Father. While the congregation prayed, struggling to find a common rhythm for their words, Ethan finally turned to Rachel. "A puppy dog? What do you make of the shell?"

"What shell?"

"In his hand."

Rachel glanced at the painting. She had grown weary with it, with Ethan, with everything. "What about it?"

"It's cracked."

"You sure?"

"Look for yourself," Ethan said, abandoning caution as the prayer came to an end and they were asked to exchange a sign of peace. "You can't miss it. But it doesn't make sense to me. If you're going to pour water into a hole, why would you use a broken shell?"

Then it came to Rachel, what she should do with the journal. It wasn't a clue, a source of information, a legacy from the person who had written it, or even a gift for the surviving brother who had found it. It was a tool, plain and simple. She would not return it to Ethan; she would put it to good use. Finally, she thought, a moment of insight in a church—it could be a first. It certainly was for her.

"You know why?" she said to Ethan, shaking his hand.

"Why?"

"Because you use whatever's available."

August 13, 2014

They say the two most dangerous words for people who grieve are "if only," but like death and taxes, they're impossible to avoid. The more I resist, the more they arrive, swarming around most of the memories I have. Since Curtis died, I've been swatting "if onlys" like flies from my thoughts. If only I hadn't felt so shitty that day. If only we had stayed home. If only I had taken a hint from the Ferris wheel. If only I hadn't been so eager for a break.

That's the thing: I just wanted a moment's peace. But "just wanted" is "if only's" partner in crime.

I just wanted to feel better. If only I had listened to Betty. That morning, my stomach was killing me, like a hand twisting from the inside.

"Why don't you just stay home and rest on the couch?" Betty said.

That's so Betty. As if Curtis would sit still for an hour. And a whole day? "It's easier to take him out," I said.

"Your call." Curtis and I had been up a full hour before her, yet with my daily struggle to wrestle him into his clothes, she managed to get ready first. "Do something for yourself," she said on the way out the door. She buzzed her hand around her head. "Maybe fix your hair. At least do your nails."

And what would Curtis do? Read the <u>Times</u>? At least it inspired Betty to pull a twenty out of her purse for me.

We went shelling. Curtis got to run around in the sand. I got his "gift," a crab shell and a gash on the hand. Still, it was better than what Curtis got in return.

My stomach grabbed me again, and I tried to lure Curtis into the food court: an ice cream for him, a hot cup of tea for me. Again, if only. As we entered the court, I heard Curtis whine. He tugged at the crotch of his shorts.

"I gotta go pee," he said.

I tried pulling him past the tables and umbrellas to the restrooms at the far end of the court.

"No, not here," he said, pulling the opposite way. "The other one."

"This is just as good. And it's closer," I said. The "other one" was at the north end of the boardwalk, just beyond the side entrance to Happy World. I could see the lure, the trap lurking ahead. Curtis was no fool.

"Go here. Then you can have an ice cream," I said, sweetening the deal. "Cookie dough with M&M's on top."

He would have none of it. "The other one!" he shouted, squishing his fly again. Faces turned our way, full of the righteous indignation of people who don't really know what's going on. Most of the time, I can plow ahead without regard to what other people think. But this time, it required energy I just didn't have.

"Fine," I said. "We'll go to the other one. And then we're coming right back."

Right.

No sooner had he come out of the men's room than he slipped out of my sight and into Happy World. I had the twenty Betty had given me. I could get a page of tickets, and maybe he would get something out of his system. And then, with the few dollars of my own, maybe I could get that tea. Sit in the shade. Watch Curtis work his way down an ice cream cone. After all, I just wanted some peace.

We started at the kiddie rides in the covered area of the park—a shrewd piece of work contrived to attract tired grandparents to the shade. And sure enough, in the daylight hours, they and their strollers made up most of the crowd.

With just two tickets, Curtis could get in one of a ring of fiberglass boats floating in a shallow circle. He was plainly too big, his knees practically banging against his chin. The attendant almost raised a fuss, but when he saw Curtis's Down syndrome face—broad as a pumpkin with forward eyes that seem ready to leap from their sockets— he turned sunburn red and mumbled something about enjoying the ride.

That Curtis did enthusiastically, gripping the wheel in complete concentration, pounding squawks from its horn as he howled along. An elderly couple, following the progress of their granddaughter—a little blondie immobilized with seasickness—were a whole lot less appreciative. The old man's video camera bobbed in synch with the boats, rising with the appearance of his little sunshine, dropping to his side as Curtis crossed his view.

With every Curtis howl, Grandma looked more disgusted. "Zoom, zoom, Gracie," she called out to her girl. "You go zoom!" There was a pride in her voice that suggested no other child could zoom quite like her granddaughter. But little Gracie remained silent. When the ride stopped, Grandma and Grandpa moved with unexpected speed to shepherd Gracie from boat to stroller; together, they darted rapidly among the rides to the carousel at the opposite end of the pavilion.

"She was slow," Curtis said. "My boat was much faster."

Curtis burned through a number of tickets on the kiddie rides and once again got bored. He wanted action; I wanted to sit down. Exasperated, I rolled my eyes. But looking up, I suddenly saw the Ferris wheel in a new light, realizing that it's just a chair in motion—and a slow motion at that. Curtis eagerly approved my suggestion. Big is good. Height is good. He grabbed my hand, and we went almost instantly from gate to gondola—there was no line at this time of day.

Once we got moving, our carriage swayed gently like a boat in calm water. The beach and the boardwalk rose and fell under us, the sounds yawing and fading like a slow lullaby. At the top, I counted forward from familiar landmarks—a corner ice cream parlor, an abandoned drive-through bank—trying to find our street, our home among so many look-alike houses. I was just beginning to feel at ease when, bam, my stomach spoke up. I squeezed my knees together and, focusing on the rocking motion, closed my eyes. When I opened them, Curtis was standing, leaning over the rail. In a flash, I saw Curtis up on his toes and nothing but empty space all around, ready to suck him into the sky.

Without a moment to think, I rushed at Curtis, pulling him back into his seat by the wrists. "What the hell are you doing?" I said wildly. "What the fuck's wrong with you?"

I regretted my words as soon as they had left my mouth. When Curtis cries, his face riots: his eyelids flutter, his lower lip trembles, his noses flares hot and red, while tears roll down the sides. "Okay," I said, wiping his face with the sleeve of my windbreaker. "That was a moment, and now it's over."

It was a phrase we shared in crisis, one I've used so often I can't remember when it started or why. But it was a handy tool for getting unstuck, for jimmying us out of tears, tantrums, or disappointments. "That was a moment, and now it's over."

I reached into my pocket: five tickets left, just enough for one of us to go on one good ride. "Tell you what," I said. "How 'bout the Rock-It Roll-It Coaster?"

If only. If only I had run out of tickets. Or suggested the flume ride. Or led him out of the park altogether.

But I didn't. I led him up to the Rock-It Roll-It Coaster—again, there wasn't much of a line—and to Leonard. I didn't know him then, of course. He was just another attendant in a red Happy World vest. Skinnier than most, with a head of shaggy hair—an animated Koosh ball on a cane.

Leonard waved Curtis forward and placed a measuring pole, like an inverted hockey stick, up to his side. "He just makes it," he said. "You riding with him?"

"I don't have enough tickets."

That was the first time I saw the smile that he would roll out at SeaSwift and the coffee shop. "I won't say anything if you won't say anything."

"Thanks," I said. "But I'll pass. I don't feel quite up to it."

"Really?" he said, opening the gate for Curtis. "It's not so bad. Its bark is worse than its bite."

"I'm good."

If only.

I am trespassing in someone else's journal. But I'm adding my voice here because his story is connected to Curtis's story; his brother's story to my story. And ours to many others'. Maybe telling them changes nothing. But I think that somehow, the pieces do fit together.

This is my piece:

The last time I saw Curtis alive, he was in the front seat of the first car with a world-eating grin on his face. The Ferris wheel was forgotten. The tears were over. A crash of guitar chords thundered over the PA, and an excitable voice asked, "Are you ready to rock?" Another blast of chords. "I can't hear you! Are you? Ready? TO ROCK?"

"I'm ready!" Curtis shouted to the mountain of tracks that towered in front of him. I shielded my eyes from the sun and followed the back of his head as the coaster rattled into motion and climbed up the hill, unsteadily, like an arthritic old man. Then it reached the top, Curtis's head eclipsed the sun, and everything old and slow dropped away as suddenly as a magician's cloak.

I found a bench by the Tilt-A-Whirl and sat down to wait, looking away from the ride. I just wanted a moment's peace.

"That was a moment, and now it's over."

No, it's not. It never will be. It keeps climbing up over the hill and into the sun, down and back again.

All these years, I'd been lying to Curtis.

That's what's over.

fathers and daughters

On what had once been a theater marquee, the letter *n* in STRAND MALL stumbled out of line, leaning drunkenly on the letter *a* for support. As promised, the front gate beneath the marquee hood was not fully closed, drawing short just a foot from the ground; the remaining gap, black as tar, was about as inviting as a wolf's jaws, but after a third look-around to be sure she wasn't seen, Rachel dropped to the ground, pushing her backpack ahead of her into the darkness. She slid in after it.

Inside, once her eyes had adjusted to the dark, various exit signs and security lights brought shapes out of the gloom, glass display cases and steel racks pinned with swimwear on either side of her; between them, a narrow walkway with an inclined floor opened into a vast womb of darkness. The floor spread wide, cluttered with shop counters and kiosks made small, almost toylike, by the great vaulted ceiling high above them. At the apex of the vault, imprisoned above an iron grill, a lone black fan chopped the air slowly. Although the theater seats, the screen, the little running lights along the aisles had been removed years ago, the space retained a gutted feeling, as if it hadn't quite finished spitting itself out.

Rachel settled the pack on her shoulder and listened. Faint voices emerged from the back—a male one, chesty and abrupt, and a female one, much less loud, like a whisper Rachel couldn't be sure she heard. She advanced toward them, her footsteps echoing in the hall, drawing closer to the "smoke shop" displays of glass pipes and plastic grinders, Zippo lighters with grinning skulls. Something clipped her shoulder, and Rachel jumped back, startled. A mannequin swayed from a length of chain suspended from the ceiling—a come-on for this season's Sea Town T-shirt, the town's name spelled out in splatters of phosphorescent paint. A few steps beyond it, a horseshoe array of stools surrounded an island of oxygen tanks and hoses. Clear masks, like fruit, hung from a wire tree topped with a sign, THE O$_2$ BAR. It promised rejuvenation and clarity of mind that could be bought in five-, ten-, or fifteen-minute sessions. *A BETTER MORNING AFTER, AFTER THE NIGHT BEFORE,* it said.

A funny proposition for a dry town, Rachel thought. She wished she had brought a flashlight, and it occurred to her that this was the second time she had forgotten to carry one: there was the fiasco with Betty, the beach, and Curtis's shells. But this time, she promised herself, what she needed to leave behind, she would leave behind. The exchange would be as sharp and quick as a ripped-off Band-Aid. In a gesture of good faith, Leonard had been released from jail. Now Stone would get the journal.

When she reached the room Stone had told her to look for, around the corner from the wall of blacklight posters, she found the people behind the voices. A young woman Rachel had seen once before sat at a card table with a bottle of Frangelico in front of her—the glass friar stood with his hands tucked into his robe, as if patient, ready to offer wisdom should the need arise. Stone stood behind the girl, similarly cross-armed but with a clear plastic cup he swirled in his hand. A weak gray light came from a computer monitor set upon a workbench along a side wall. The computer's cooling fan whirred softly; the old theater's great fan made a slow and steady *chop-chop* sound.

Rachel removed the bag from her shoulders, holding it from the strap like a severed head by the hair.

"Have a seat," Stone said. He nodded to a folding chair leaning against the table—a guest too tired to stand on its feet.

The chair squealed as Rachel opened it. The table was scarred with random box-knife cuts and fragments of packing tape. The room, and everything in it, felt disposable—to be used, then thrown away. "This is yours too, this place?"

"It's all his," the girl said, her face obscured by her hair. Stone nudged her shoulder with the knuckles of his drink hand. "Ours," she said.

"This is my daughter, Diana," said Stone. "Diana, this is Rachel Leary. She works for me at the Playground. Someday she might work for you."

"Not likely," Rachel said. "I got other plans."

"Stranger things have happened," Stone said. "My staff is filled with people who thought they would move on to bigger things."

Rachel wondered how long he'd been pulling at the bottle. Kid stuff: sweet and heavy. A smell like burnt pancake syrup hung in the air. She wanted to blow it all away: the smell, the dark, the tension. "What I don't get," she said, "what I can't figure out, is how you moved Jason."

For the first time, Diana looked up. The gray light didn't do her any favors. Hints of smeared mascara—from tears?—hid in the creases along her nose. It may have been the makeup, but something about her looked shriveled. Rachel wondered what Jason had seen in her. But then, Rachel hadn't been part of that special moment—the threatening drunks, the retrieved soda cup—that changed everything. She marveled that one moment, like the push of a button, could reset the world. Was that the power of fear or courage?

"You don't know what you're talking about," Diana said.

"I read the journal," Rachel said. "From Happy World to the beach. I figure he must have been, what, at least a hundred sixty, a hundred seventy pounds? And carried over the boardwalk too."

"Must be a magic journal," Stone said, "if the dead can write in it."

Rachel struggled not to smile. "So Jason was at the park that night?"

"Dad," Diana said, trying to pry the drink from her father's hand. He pushed her back into her chair.

"She's bluffing," he said. "Watch. Watch and learn. That's what you're here for."

"I figure," Rachel said, tracing stars on the table with her finger, "what would I do? I'm Diana. I'm in a place I shouldn't be with a boy I shouldn't be with. Now he's on the ground, and he isn't moving. I check his breathing, his pulse. Nothing. What do I do? Call an ambulance? Call the police? No, I go straight to the top. I call Daddy."

"Ask her if she brought the journal," Stone said to Diana. "Go ahead."

Her head down again, Diana's hair fell like a curtain across her face.

"Something went wrong with the Magic Carpet," Rachel continued. "It had worked before—in the summer. But it was winter. Jason was smart, very smart, but he hadn't accounted for the weather." She looked straight at Diana. "The freezing cold."

"Ask for the damn journal," Stone hissed.

"You ask," Diana said.

"I don't care which of you asks," Rachel said. "I'll make a deal with either one of you."

Stone took another sip. "A deal? You think there's going to be a deal?"

"That's what I'm here for."

The fan *chop-chopped* in the silence. Rachel wondered if a little green ribbon was attached to its grill.

"You're going to give the journal to us," Stone said softly. "And I mean, give. You know why?"

Rachel shook her head.

"Because we're friends, Rachel. We're all friends here." He frowned into his cup. "I'd offer you a drink, but you're underage. And this is a dry town, after all."

"Some friend," Rachel said. "I've got my own people to look after."

"Let's be real. One way or another, I'm going to get that journal. You know that, right?"

"Maybe."

"There's no 'maybe' about it. You know that. Why do this?"

He spread out his arms, encompassing what, Rachel wondered: the cruddy room, the cruddy table? His daughter? This night? This world?

"Why fight?" he asked, dropping his arms.

"Because I owe it to my brother. And to Jason. And Ethan. Leonard."

Stone waved his hand dismissively, swishing drink out of his cup. "You owe them nothing," he said. He wiped his fingers on his shirt. "Leonard? The kid was stoned. Did he tell you that?"

"In his way."

"And Jason, he was reckless."

"Maybe. He slipped up. But not from the jetty. Was there water in his lungs?"

Stone brushed that aside too. "It wasn't drowning. It was a contusion or a concussion or some such thing. A blow to the head." He punctuated his recollection by slapping his thigh. "That's what it was. From the rocks."

"Stop it," Diana said. "Let's get this over with."

"That's what we're here for, sweetheart," Stone said.

"Rocks, my ass," Rachel said. "A magic carpet ride that went wrong."

The room was too dark to detect any change of color in Stone's face. He filled the pause before he spoke, not with a sip, but with a long, cold look into his cup. "Bullshit," he said. "There's no evidence of that."

"If there wasn't," Rachel said, "you wouldn't have asked me to come here."

"It was an accident, for Christ's sake." He caught himself, waving his free hand as if erasing a chalkboard. "If such a thing had happened, which it did not."

"He didn't accidentally drop his own body in the ocean, did he?"

"That's just what I was trying to say," Stone said, sliding into a chair beside his daughter. "That's responsibility. You, of all people, should appreciate that."

Rachel gripped her backpack. "What does that mean?"

"Judgment," Stone said with some heat. "Look at you." He pushed the Frangelico bottle to one side, opening his hands to encourage confidences. "You're hurt. You're in pain. You're looking for someone to blame. But come on. Tell me something. Your brother should never have gone on that ride alone, right? Don't tell me that's never crossed your mind."

"All the time," Rachel said. "But it doesn't matter. He was old enough. He was tall enough."

"He was *retarded.*" Stone dropped his hands on the table. "You were the responsible one. You were the one supposed to exercise judgment. If only you had."

"If only the ride hadn't malfunctioned."

"You're doing it again—making stuff up. That's grief talking, not brains." He tapped his temple. "But I'm not here to judge. No, I'm not." Again, a sip from his cup. "Look. There are two kinds of people in this world. Most of them are weak, needy, always waiting for someone else to tell them what to do. To set things right. To make things work. You know that. I mean, look at Chuck Waters. Decent guy, but come on. A hopeless case."

"And you give them hope?"

"I give them work," Stone said. He looked quizzically at his cup, saw that it was empty, and reached for the bottle. "Tell me, where are your friends? Where's Ethan?"

"I don't know."

"I do. He's at home. Safe." Stone looked Rachel in the eye. "Forgive me for getting personal, but . . . where's your mother in all this? How long are you going to carry her? Who's the adult? Who's the child?"

He's really drunk, Rachel thought. "What's this have to do with you?"

"We're the other kind, Rachel. Don't you see? The kind who take responsibility. Who make decisions. Who think things through—who think and take action. We clean up the messes other people leave behind." He draped his arm around Diana. She squirmed free, lifting the weight of his arm over and away from her.

Stone laughed. "I wonder if you two were switched at birth. You," he said, pointing an unsteady finger at Rachel, "you I can see running this place. You"—this time nodding to Diana—"you I worry about. But you're what I've got to work with."

"I wouldn't trade places for all the money in the world," Rachel said. "I just want to get the hell out of here."

Diana lifted her head. Streaked mascara made her look like a jungle cat. "So what's stopping you?" she asked.

Rachel couldn't think of anything to say. She stared into the table as if the scars would speak for her.

"That thing with Jason," Stone said. "If he had been found in the park, you know what that would mean?"

"Your park would close," Rachel said. "You would lose money."

"People would lose *jobs.* The town would lose taxes. The shore would lose tourists. It might be years before we recovered. If we ever recovered."

"You don't know that."

"Really? Think, Rachel. Use the gifts God gave you. Why should the many suffer for the one? And for what? He was dead. There was no bringing him back."

"What about the truth?"

"Truth is what we make of it," Stone said, finishing his drink. "Sometimes we make tough calls, hard choices. But who has the right to judge us?"

"I don't know."

"No one, Rachel." Stone rose from his seat, taking up a stance behind his daughter. She seemed to shrink under him. "You don't even have to hand the journal to us," Stone said. "Just put it on the table and walk away. You never have to see me pick it up. And you can tell your friends anything you want. I forced it from you. I threatened your mother. I promised not to press charges against that Washington kid. Or you can make it simple. In all the confusion, you dropped it on the boardwalk by accident and don't know what happened to it. You have no idea."

She could run, Rachel thought. She could race out the door, off the boardwalk, away from Sea Town. She could jump into a car with Leonard, and together, they could hit the road with whatever cash they could scrape together, making the great getaway Leonard said he wanted. She could almost feel the air whistling around them, racing.

And then? Where would they go? There was always that long black wall at the end of every daydream of escape. Rachel hadn't the will to paint a picture on it she could believe in.

"I hope you read it," Rachel said, reaching into her backpack. "Both of you." She looked at Diana, whose eyes followed the journal from the pack to the table. "Jason loved you, you know."

"He was so young," Stone said.

"And me, I loved Curtis."

"Only natural."

"I wish it were," said Rachel.

Stone had said she could just walk away, and now that she had produced the journal, it was as if she had already left. Impatient to see what was inside, Stone cracked the notebook open, squinting into pages he turned in the dark.

"Shit," he said. "I should've brought a flashlight."

Rachel grinned: he was no smarter than she was. She crossed her arms and watched.

But then Diana reached under her chair. "I have something," she said, dropping a purse on the table. Rushing, she withdrew objects by the careless handful: loose change and wadded bills, sticks of lipstick and mascara, a bronze ring of keys—and, just before the triumphant rise of a miniature flashlight she proudly clicked into life, a small, heart-shaped locket on a silver chain. It skittered onto the table with a snare drum splash.

The Stones couldn't wait to read the journal, their heads side-by-side, would-be Siamese twins joined at the shoulder. Diana held the small flashlight like a spear, and their faces glowed, ghostly and intense, in the light reflected from the book. Curiosity, anxiety, satisfaction—all these burned in their expressions, but Rachel understood the moment for what it was: a distraction.

Her fingers sucked the locket into her palm without a sound, then slipped it into her pocket. The Stones continued to read, oblivious. Their greedy absorption of the journal annoyed her. "I'm not leaving empty-handed," Rachel said.

Father and daughter looked up at her, startled, as if they had forgotten she was still there.

"I'm taking this bottle."

Returning his attention to the journal, Bobby Stone waved his hand magnanimously. "Help yourself," he said, "to whatever's left of it. Just, you know, be discreet."

Rachel left the way she had come, passing the oxygen counter where, she guessed, Diana would drag her father before they left for home. As Rachel had once spoon-fed baby Curtis, Diana would fuss over her father, attending to his needs. She pictured Diana, a slight girl, navigating her father's bearlike bulk toward the counter. She would settle him onto a stool and, with one hand steadying his chin, struggle to put an oxygen mask over his face. Rachel anticipated the hiss of gas from the tank, the sighs from Diana, and the way the two sounds would mix, indistinguishable.

Through the narrow bite of the entrance gate, Rachel crawled out of the mall, then pulled herself to her feet. Nothing had changed. The streetlamps along the boardwalk bowed their heads in martial order, marching north and south into the distance. The gulls, without much to fight over, swirled quietly above the storefronts. On the beach, the surf crashed, withdrew, and crashed again as it always had.

Rachel withdrew the locket from her pants and opened it. *JW + DS.* Jason Waters plus Diana Stone. What did it equal? An incomplete equation. But at least there was no inscription promising undying love. That would have been awful. With a small but satisfying click between thumb and finger, she closed the locket.

How fragile, Rachel thought. Out of nowhere, she pictured Sledge Leary, the man with the iron hands. A powerful man who wanted nothing more than a little peace, a home away from the living dead. She paused under the old marquee, sliding her pack from her shoulders. What would Sledge Leary do? She pulled the Frangelico bottle out from her bag. After a quick swirl of its dregs and a small bow to the friar, Rachel smashed it at the foot of the Strand.

The gulls squalled at the sudden explosion. A scent of hazelnut rose in the air; the broken pieces of glass sparkled with lamplight, a minor galaxy of amber stars.

Someone will clean up this mess before dawn, Rachel thought. *Someone will have to.* After all, this was America's number one family resort.

chapter eighteen

fire

The fire leapt and licked, jumped and gnawed at the amusement park; it did not burn so much as bite, eating away at Happy World.

"You know what happens now?" Leonard said. "Everyone's going to say, 'This is our 9/11, the day Happy World burned down.' There'll be posters and T-shirts: 'August 14, 2014. Always remember.'"

He was probably right, Rachel thought: remembering would be a collective effort. This time, commemoration wouldn't be solitary. It wouldn't be her and Betty with a sack of shells, or Ethan with a marker in his hand. This time, the whole town would not only remember, but insist on it.

Leonard squeezed her hand. "They're going to come for us," he said, dropping his voice. "We should go. Now."

"No," she said. "Too suspicious."

"What about Ethan? You think he—"

"No."

"Glad you're so sure. He probably thinks it was you. You think he'll say so?" When Rachel didn't respond, he added, "They'll look for enemies."

"Then they'll be looking the wrong way."

He searched her face. "You know who did this?"

"Maybe," she said, drawing her arm around him. "Sledge Leary?"

"I wish. But this ain't a comic book," he said. "Seriously. Is it someone close to us?"

"Close to us?"

With the collapse of the Happy World facade, the fire, as if it had run out of rage, began to dim. Rolls of black smoke replaced the flames, and the beach crowds began to disperse.

"Close to us?" Rachel said again. "Yes and no."

It seemed awkward, reckless, and just plain stupid, but earlier in the day, Rachel had sought Diana out again. Swiping the locket from her had been a consolation prize, a little way of feeling less small at the time. But in the morning, clutching the locket in her hand, Rachel felt the weight of the thing Diana had kept with her, her secret all these months: her way of remembering.

Finding her was easy. There she was, just as Jason had described her, in the booth underneath the lonely astronaut, her face as pale as the moon. "Here," Rachel had said without fuss, setting the locket down and letting the chain run, like silver water, into a puddle on the counter.

Strangely, Diana didn't seem surprised. "I was up half the night looking for it," Diana said. "I turned my bedroom inside out." But she did not pick it up. She did not touch it.

"It's all yours," Rachel said.

"Funny," Diana said. "My father says that all the time. Ever since I was a little girl. He'd take me by the hand and drag me to the middle of Happy World, in the middle of the crowd, and lift me up. So I could see."

"'Someday all this will be yours'?"

"Something like that," Diana said. She looked at the locket. "Where did you find it?"

"I didn't find it," Rachel said. "I stole it. Last night. You were a bit distracted."

"The journal."

"You read it?"

"Last night."

"The other half of the night?" Rachel asked. "When you weren't looking for the locket?"

"You think it's a joke?" Diana said.

"No," Rachel said. "That's why I came back. With this." She pushed the locket forward.

Diana shook her head. Her face was in the shadows of the booth, but her eyes gleamed. With what, Rachel wondered. Tears? Rage?

"Give it to Ethan," Diana said.

"But Jason gave it to you," Rachel said. "It's yours."

"This is mine," Diana said, lifting her chin. "This booth, this boardwalk, Happy World."

"All yours?"

"I've paid for it," Diana said.

"So did Jason," Rachel said. She thought, *So did Curtis and Ethan and Leonard and I.* And there were others: Betty, Chuck Waters, his wife. Anyone who had known and loved Curtis, anyone who had known and loved Jason.

Rachel had taken the locket again, this time under Diana's

watchful eyes, which—Rachel considered in retrospect, her head pressed against the warmth of Leonard's chest—had gleamed with something like fire.

"I think we know who did this," Rachel said, "but I wouldn't say we're close."

chapter nineteen

going

The ceiling of the Atlantic City Bus Terminal was too low for the station's size, an anxious weight overhead that seemed to compress travelers, as if squeezing might accelerate them through their arrivals or departures. Most were departing. Arrivals came in Lincolns and Lexuses, Rachel reasoned. Departures took the bus.

Ethan was among the departing. He slouched in a fiberglass seat with a backpack in his lap, staring blankly at a television suspended from the ceiling.

"Where you headed?" she said, taking a seat next to his. The air smelled of Old Spice and disinfectant.

"New York," Ethan said without looking up. "How'd you know I'd be here?"

"You can't drive," Rachel said. When she and Leonard had knocked at his door that morning, a very weary Mr. Waters said he hadn't seen him all night. He assumed Ethan was with his mother, but said that he had been debating the merits of reporting him as missing, the bitch.

"Where in New York?"

Ethan shrugged. "Manhattan."

Rachel tucked her legs beneath her. "You'll have to do better than that," she said. "You'll need an address. You got one?"

His clothes wrinkled, his hair flopped carelessly over his eyes, Ethan looked deflated, a balloon that had lost its gas. "I'll call her when I get there."

"She doesn't know you're coming, does she?"

Ethan didn't answer. As Rachel considered what she might say next, the local news came on the television. The big story was the same as it had been for several days: the devastating fire that had razed Happy World. Officials had found evidence of arson; in a shocking development, police were talking to "persons of interest" in the Stone family itself. Sea Town's mayor offered a brief comment, wishing to assure citizens and guests alike that Sea Town was now as it always had been, a safe place for all, a family town.

Ethan drew his backpack tighter in his arms. "They're coming after us," he said. "Me and my dad."

"You're not part of the Stone family," Rachel said. "Not now. Never were."

"That's reassuring." He turned away from her, curling fetally in his chair, his eyes open but remote. "Where's Jason's journal? I want it back."

"It's gone. Anyway, you don't need it. You have his heart."

"Very funny."

"Give me your hand," Rachel said. "Go ahead."

"You're not part of my family, either."

"And that's a bad thing? Come on."

Without force, as if charmed like a snake from a fakir's basket, Ethan's hand rose from his side, his fingers ready for Rachel's grip. But she didn't give him her hand. Instead, she turned his palm up and into it poured the locket and its long silver chain.

"What's this?"

"Jason's heart," Rachel said. "The one he gave to Diana."

Ethan opened the locket; he read the inscription. "How'd you get this?"

"Diana gave it to me."

"She didn't want to keep it?"

"I think she's letting go of things," Rachel said. She considered the sacrifice. If Diana cared enough for the locket to carry it with her, wouldn't she steal private moments to admire it? Moments when no one was looking, no one was around, when her father wasn't over her shoulder? This would be her thing, hers alone—and that would make it precious. Rachel pictured Diana tracing and retracing her steps, searching the floor of the Strand Mall, turning her bedroom inside out. "What are you looking for?" her parents might ask, hovering in the doorway. And Diana would have to answer, "Nothing. I'm not looking for anything," or make up a thing that meant nothing to her at all, lies piled onto loss. Rachel pitied the girl. Right now, she could be sitting in the little room where detectives put the pieces together: Happy World. Hot fire. Cold daughter.

Rachel had put it together on the beach, huddled with Leonard for warmth, watching the flames. He was more precious to her than anything she could imagine, more than any shell could be to Curtis, any boyfriend could be to Betty. More than a father could be to Diana? Rachel had hugged Leonard as if she could swallow him whole and said yes, they knew who set the fire and no, it was not someone close. Yes, because they knew her. No, because it wasn't possible for Diana to stand with them.

Jason had left her a locket; her father was going to leave Diana a world—it probably began to burn the minute she sat alone with the journal, the flames rising with the voice that came alive on each page.

Rachel could see Diana in the dark with a match and a memory she wanted to leave behind. The more Rachel tried to scratch the picture from her mind, the more solid it became. "Careful who you disturb," Diana once said. Maybe she had said it again to her father. She was almost certainly saying it to herself.

"Thanks," Ethan said, pocketing the jewelry. "My mom will be surprised." Color returned to his face. "You want to come with me?"

"It's tempting." Rachel looked around. Even at seven in the morning, there was a sizeable crowd getting ready to leave. They looked wretched, beaten—and probably were, in the sense that they had lost much of what they had. Winning gamblers didn't go home by bus. They returned with the cars they had arrived in. Or they hired a car. Or flew. Losers scraped up what they could to take the bus. In fact, the terminal was one of the last places in the city with pay phones. So many of the calls were the same: "I'm stuck in AC," they would say, amazed by their inexplicable circumstances. "Can you buy me a ticket?" But no matter how desperate the situation, they were always washed. They may have lost everything, and many were still dizzily drunk, yet they had managed to clean up. Their hair was almost always wet, and when you came close to them, the alcohol on their breath was masked by the apple scent of shampoo.

"My mom's not coming back," Ethan said flatly, as if the only wonder was that it had taken him so long to see it.

"I'm sorry," Rachel said. "My mom's going to move in with her boyfriend."

"What about you?"

"Mrs. K has a room for me. I'm welcome to it—as long as I take classes."

"College?"

"Atlantic Cape Community," Rachel said. "Close enough."

Ethan nodded his head. "My mom says she wants to go back to school."

"To find herself."

"How'd you know?"

"That's what people say," Rachel said, stretching her legs out, "when they're getting lost." The news had moved on to the next segment, two anchors sipping coffee, sharing a gentle chuckle over the most amusing personal interest story ever—at least since yesterday. "What time's your bus?"

Ethan pulled a ticket from his pocket. "Seven forty-five," he said.

"Want to get a bite to eat? Leonard's waiting in the car. We were thinking maybe Rose's for cheesecake."

"Cheesecake?"

"And coffee."

"I've never had a cup of coffee," Ethan said. "I always thought it was one of those things adults like because they're supposed to, not because it's good."

"No," Rachel said, "coffee's good." Across the floor of the

terminal, waiting ticket holders slouched on benches or lounged under television screens. A classic rock station played over the PA—somebody was going to break somebody's heart tonight. Few people spoke. Who was in the mood? But once they were on the bus with a cup of coffee in them, Rachel guessed, they would open up. Strangers would turn to strangers, and while they wouldn't be specific, they would talk about their losses. Strangers understood without explanations. They would share tips about point spreads and twenty-one, about where the loose slots were and which casinos gave the most generous comps. They would talk about Blue Men and white tigers and Cirque du Soleil, about the best shows and the great, the truly greatest entertainers—the best were dead and gone, they'd agree, leaving memories more brilliantly lit than anything they'd see again in their lives. The Garden State Parkway and the New Jersey Turnpike would race outside their windows, and time would accelerate even faster. On a bus among strangers, sitting still and moving on were one and the same.

"Coffee's the thing," said Rachel. "I've grown to like it. Really." She got up from her seat. "Join us?"

"Is there time?" Ethan asked, examining his ticket. "Will I make my bus?"

"Probably not," Rachel said, offering her hand. "Let me take your bag for you."

For a moment, Ethan seemed as frozen in space as the television hanging above them, flickering. Then he stirred, returning the ticket to his pocket. "I'll need a lot of milk and sugar," he said.

"Whatever it takes."

"All right." With his bag slung over his shoulder, Ethan

shifted himself forward. Rachel took his hand and helped him to his feet.

Outside the terminal, the sun had risen just enough to chase off the morning damp. It felt reassuring after the excessive, air-conditioned chill inside. Leonard waited for them in his car, idling at the curb.

"C'mon," he said, leaning across the front seat to yell out the passenger window. "I'm in a tow zone."

Rachel tossed Ethan's bag through the back window.

"Hey," Leonard said, "be careful." Rachel wasn't sure which concerned him more: his wreck of a car that was, nonetheless, a source of pride, or the grocery bag of shells on the back seat that had been the bulk of Curtis's collection. Last night, the plan had been to go to one of the nearly deserted beaches at the south end of Sea Town, where they would stand on a jetty to say a few words for Jason and Curtis, then return the shells to the sea. Last night, it had seemed like the right thing to do—poetic and honorable. Now, in the light of day, Rachel wasn't so sure. The idea seemed corny or worse. It felt false.

"Let's get something to eat," Rachel said, opening the door. She climbed in the front and gave Leonard a kiss; Ethan got in back. The car reeked of cigarette smoke and fast-food wrappers, but Rachel didn't mind. It was Leonard's car. It was all good. She tapped the hula girl on the dash to make her hips dance.

"What about the beach thing?" Leonard asked, pulling away from the curb. "You know, the shells?"

"Forget the shells," Rachel said. "They're not going any-where." Rose's was on the other side of the island, just a block from the Atlantic City boardwalk and yet light-years from the gamblers' orbit, a quiet refuge from barking slot machine bells and blinding casino floor shows. At seven fifteen in the morning, there was no traffic to speak of. Stray newspaper pages blew across otherwise empty roads, and traffic lights changed for their own amusement. In this open lace of streets and breezes, Leonard savored the opportunity to pick up speed. His engine roared as if delighted to be set free, and Ethan, leaning into the gap between the front seats, cheered Leonard on, encouraging him to go, go, go.

Rachel felt the familiar urge to steal. But in a speeding car with her boys, there was nothing to take that she didn't already have. Her left hand found Leonard's knee, her right, the escape of an open window. Among her free fingers the rushing air whipped and played. Rachel made a grab for it, letting the wind take her hand.

She held on tight.

acknowledgments

It may be true that writing a novel is a lonely process. But publishing a book—giving birth to it in the world—demands the skills, the talents, and the stubborn goodwill of many gifted people. I want to express my gratitude to those who helped put this book in your hands: Marcy Posner, Laura Godwin, Julia Sooy, Maggie Reagan, April Ward, Ana Deboo, Sherri Schmidt, and the people of Henry Holt. Thank you!